Confessions of a
21st-Century Martyr

Confessions of a 21st-Century Martyr

PAUL FITZGERALD BUCKLEY

Text copyright © 2021 by Paul Fitzgerald Buckley

Cover art copyright © 2021 by
John Buckley, https://studionumio.com
Cover photo: Rene Böhmer (@qrenep) | Unsplash Photo
Cover design uses imagee by BiZkettE1 - www.freepik.com

All rights reserved. Published in the United States by SaviorLabs, Boxford, MA.

Unless otherwise noted, Scripture quotations are taken from Holy Bible: New Living Translation Tyndale House Publishers. (2015). Used by permission. All rights reserved.

Scripture denoted by (ESV) is taken from The Holy Bible, English Standard Version. Copyright © 2007 by Crossway Bibles, a publishing ministry of Good News Publishers. Used by permission. All rights reserved.

ISBN 979-8-473-97283-2

Imprint: Independently published

The text of this book is set in 12-point Verdigris MVB Pro Text. Interior design by Paul Parisi

Printed in the United States of America

Table of Contents

Preface

This book is written to bring to life the values and vision of a Christian worldview through a story. It isn't a technical book but does contain copious technical footnotes for further study and reflection. My recommendation is first to read through it as a work of fiction. Read it to enjoy the story and get to know the main characters. If you are then interested in digging in more, you can review the footnotes for further reflection and learning opportunities. (The footnotes are offered either from the perspective of the actual author or from the perspective of the fictional author. The context should help you figure out who is writing.)

This book is a work of fiction. All the characters are fictional, and all the scenarios are hypothetical. They are not meant to be prophetic nor even the best representation of what might happen. It is written as fiction with a central purpose – to envision Christians for what *could be* as God's kingdom advances in our world.

I have taken some liberties in writing this book to best illustrate what could be. These include somewhat fantastical possibilities like aliens and the Nephilim, compressing the massive growth of God's kingdom into one lifetime, and imagining a working union of all Nicene Christianity. These liberties are taken only to illustrate essential truths or accentuate critical values that convey a Christian worldview. They are appropriately footnoted with the needed qualifications. I trust they will be taken as intended.

I hope this book will inform and inspire you with a compelling vision of the Christian life. I hope you will see what the kingdom of God can look like when it affects every sphere of life.

Paul Fitzgerald Buckley
Haverhill, MA, USA, Christmas, 2020

i

Introduction

My dad wrote this book to help those facing life-threatening trials. Our current time of tribulation – maybe "The Tribulation" – tests our hearts and threatens to overwhelm us.[1] My dad wrote this as he was facing some of the worst stuff that any human can face. He wanted me to make sure this got out to as many people as possible after his death. He and my family hope this will help you somehow.

My name is Matthias. I am the oldest son of Lucas and Abby Sullivan.[2] I am married with three grown children. My dad grew up at the beginning of this century right around the time things started to get out of control.

He was born way back at the beginning of this century as the firstborn of my Latina Abuelita, Isabel Muñoz Garcia, and my Irish American Grampa, Sean Sullivan. He graduated high school in that historic year that the coronavirus pandemic hit the world. It left a mark on pretty much everyone, including Dad. He went off to college and jumped into the fray of society as it bounced between the right and the left and came unraveled

---

[1] "Immediately after the tribulation of those days the sun will be darkened, and the moon will not give its light, and the stars will fall from heaven, and the powers of the heavens will be shaken. Then will appear in heaven the sign of the Son of Man, and then all the tribes of the earth will mourn, and they will see the Son of Man coming on the clouds of heaven with power and great glory. And he will send out his angels with a loud trumpet call, and they will gather his elect from the four winds, from one end of heaven to the other. (Matthew 24:29–31 ESV)

[2] Many of the names have been altered for the protection of those living.

in the process. My dad tried everything but God during college. After graduating and going on to grad school, he started searching for something that might be better than the constant dysphoria that seemed to saturate everything.

He made friends with a fellow grad student named Ryan, who remained one of his best friends throughout his life. Ryan risked arrest himself to be there for my dad's final days. This dear friend and his loving church made an imprint on Dad, and through their influence and hours and hours of late nights explaining the Christian faith, Dad came to believe in Christ, was baptized, and never looked back.

He also met my mom at that church. Her story is equally wild. She started in a Christian home. The tumult of the time, the weakness of western Christianity, and Mom's own rebellion led her into plenty of wild soul-searching before God called her back. They got married in the same year that the Council on Church Unity met, so all-in-all, it was a pretty big year.

Dad had a great career as a research scientist for a biotech research lab. That lab was the dream of some like-minded Christian entrepreneurs and scientists who wanted to help people for Jesus. After twenty years of outstanding research, including finding a cure for many viral illnesses, he left to become a local parish pastor.

His work as a pastor put him in contact with lots of great stuff worldwide. We experienced the most fantastic time of Christian growth and influence since Christ himself walked the earth. What an incredible 50 years it was! The Christlikeness and power of the reunited church seemed to catch the world on fire. We all watched as just about every Jewish person we knew came to faith in Yeshua HaMashiach.[3] It was like a living dream. Dad, and many of us, were an integral part of all that. We are so grateful for him, and all that God did during that time.

But, as you know, we woke up from that dream when things took a bad turn with the rise of "The Messengers," as they call them. We know them as "The Deceivers."[4] They showed up like gods and goddesses of mythology, arising to lead us to a supposed higher form of humanity. They were the result of integrating artificial intelligence into humans. They are a modern form of the Nephilim, the evil product of men and fallen angels.[5] "The Messengers" supposedly had a special pipeline to

---

[3] "Now if the Gentiles were enriched because the people of Israel turned down God's offer of salvation, think how much greater a blessing the world will share when they finally accept it… For since their rejection meant that God offered salvation to the rest of the world, their acceptance will be even more wonderful. It will be life for those who were dead!" (Romans 11:12,15)

[4] "This man will come to do the work of Satan with counterfeit power and signs and miracles. He will use every kind of evil deception to fool those on their way to destruction, because they refuse to love and accept the truth that would save them. So God will cause them to be greatly deceived, and they will believe these lies." (2 Thessalonians 2:9–11)

[5] "Then the people began to multiply on the earth, and daughters were born to them. The sons of God saw the beautiful women and took any they wanted as their wives. Then the LORD said, "My Spirit will not put up with humans for such a long time, for they are only mortal flesh. In the future, their normal lifespan will be no more than 120 years." In those days, and for some time after, giant Nephilites lived on the earth, for whenever the

visitations from alien beings who offered themselves as benevolent cosmic guides for a pathway to a better humanity. Their pathway is to a humanity further away from God's design and deeper into evil. Their denial of Jesus Christ was a dead giveaway for their demonic origins.[6]

---

sons of God had intercourse with women, they gave birth to children who became the heroes and famous warriors of ancient times." (Genesis 6:1–4)

"So they spread this bad report about the land among the Israelites: 'The land we traveled through and explored will devour anyone who goes to live there. All the people we saw were huge. We even saw giants there, the descendants of Anak. Next to them we felt like grasshoppers, and that's what they thought, too!'" (Numbers 13:32–33)

Although the Bible can support the reappearance of the Nephilim, this teaching is not indisputable. For further study on this possibility consider Heiser, M. S. (2015). Unseen Realm. Lexham Press.

[6] "Dear friends, do not believe everyone who claims to speak by the Spirit. You must test them to see if the spirit they have comes from God. For there are many false prophets in the world. This is how we know if they have the Spirit of God: If a person claiming to be a prophet acknowledges that Jesus Christ came in a real body, that person has the Spirit of God. But if someone claims to be a prophet and does not acknowledge the truth about Jesus, that person is not from God. Such a person has the spirit of the Antichrist, which you heard is coming into the world and indeed is already here. But you belong to God, my dear children. You have already won a victory over those people, because the Spirit who lives in you is greater than the spirit who lives in the world. Those people belong to this world, so they speak from the world's viewpoint, and the world listens to them. But we belong to God, and those who know God listen to us. If they do not belong to God, they do not listen to us. That is how we know if someone has the Spirit of truth or the spirit of deception." (1 John 4:1–6)

Their deception was powerful and complete; through the use of miracles and superhuman insight and predictions it didn't take too long for many folks to fall for their story. There was resistance and some very destructive conflicts. A number of important cities were nuked with neutron bombs. The Deceivers' victory and the capitulation to their creed by every major country and every major religion, except Christianity, was complete within a few years. The Union of Sovereign Peoples, USP, followed. Their new laws against "Misanthropic Speech and Religion" spelled doom, humanly speaking, for my dad and so many of us.

Dad was one of the first to die. He was followed by thousands upon thousands. No one knows the final tally, but it will probably end up in the billions if it doesn't stop. We know it will stop the instant our good and glorious God has planned it to stop. And God will work his perfect mercy and justice for all to see.

I think God allowed my dad to be one of the first to die and the author of this "Confession" to somehow give all of us both the instruction and the inspiration we need. Many of us will likely follow him in martyrdom, should the Lord wait to return. It is my prayer, along with my whole family and parish, that you would find the strength to "trust in the LORD and do good" through this precious book.

Matthias Sullivan, New Boston Megalopolis, USP (NAU)

You can find more copies of this book through the Christian dark matrix known as "the catacombs." The address is ever-changing to avoid the authorities. But if you know where to find

the catacombs and type in "Confessions of a 21st-Century Martyr," it should show up.

Chapter 1: First Things

Monday, August 8

Well, here I am, believe it or not. Me, Lucas Sullivan, no hero, no celebrity, just me, in prison awaiting my likely execution.[7] What a crazy day it was today. I would never have dreamed it even five years ago. But it is happening, and so I begin my journal of my last days on this earth as I've known it. May God bless it even in some small way as he has Augustine's book of confessions that has gripped my heart all these years.[8] So, here goes.

What can I say about today? Well, it was shocking, sobering, a little surreal, but definitely life changing. The judge was there with her black robes and gavel behind that big wooden bench. The lawyers for the government were there. They seemed like nice enough people. My lawyer was with me and my two boys and a bunch of friends from the church, along with my younger brother. It was a pretty dramatic scene.

The chief lawyer for the government was sharp and eloquent. He reviewed my case and recommended the "final solution," as they call it. It isn't final in my view. And it definitely isn't a solution. But, anyhow, that's what he recommended. Scary.

He did a really good job of imploring me to change my mind and to pledge to keep my "hurtful and hateful" views private

---

[7] The USP uses multiple methods to deal with non-compliant criminals including brain implants, drug therapy, surgery and termination of life.

[8] Augustine, (1961). Confessions. Baltimore: Penguin Books.

1

and thus avoid the severe sentence. It was hard to sit through. He talked about all the good things that are going on since the Union of Sovereign Peoples was formed. He spoke of the necessity of curtailing all public communications that would undermine the Union so that it could truly flourish for the good of all mankind. He covered the history of the past 70 years and the polarization and civil wars that led to so much destruction. It kinda sounded like it was all my fault. I wish he had covered the other side of the story. But that is why I have this journal.

He made a good case for me keeping my mouth shut and avoiding the death sentence. Why not just keep my opinions to myself, stay in my lane and just get along? Why should I give up all that I have for a personal religious preference? Isn't peace and mutual respect and economic and community flourishing more important than personal opinions? He said I had some time to think it over before the sentence would be carried out. It seemed pretty final when the judge hit that gavel. But, I know they want to avoid having to use the "final solution" with people like me. He made a clear case that weighs on me pretty heavily.

Definitely, lots to think about.

Tuesday, August 9th

Well, I have been thinking a lot about it and praying too. On the one side, I totally get the desire to avoid strife and the destruction that so often comes from disagreements. I would much rather have peace than return to what I saw as a young man. What a crazy time that was! It's a wonder we survived. I am so grateful for meeting Abby back then and the two of us making it safely through "The Cataclysm," as they call it. That time changed everything.

So, the importance of peace makes sense. So does living long enough to watch my grandchildren grow up and be successful. And keeping my local parish out of trouble as much as possible makes sense. And avoiding bringing scandal to the Christian name is worth something too. And especially seeing my sweet Abby again, holding her hand, hearing her melodic voice, looking in those ocean-blue eyes, talking about life, laughing, walking together, celebrating birthdays and holidays with the kids and all our friends. How can I let go of her and all that? What if this is all just about my pride and stubbornness? Please, God, help me.

As much as I love peace, as much as I want to obey the authorities and see everybody flourish, as much as I love Abby and the kids and our friends and our parish, I can't trade truth and goodness and glory for these precious things. If I do, I will only be living a lie and leading others to do the same – it will all be hollow and sooner or later come crashing down. I know this isn't pride because I have too much to lose personally. I feel humiliated by the whole thing. But it isn't ultimately about me, and that clarifies so much.

O God, help me. Help me remember these things. Help me feel these things. Keep me from my own weakness and fallenness. Protect me from the enemies of my soul – my own sin, the devil and this mixed-up world. Lead me in the way everlasting. *"Whom have I in heaven but you? I desire you more than anything on earth. My health may fail, and my spirit may grow weak, but God remains the strength of my heart; he is mine forever."* (Psalm 73:25–26)

O God, show me your glory! O God, defeat the doubts of my heart. Strengthen me for what lies ahead, convince my mind and heart, and my body that you are truly greater than all because you are the creator, sustainer, and object of all that there is. You alone are the living God! Help me, I pray!

Wednesday, August 10th

The best night of sleep I've had in a while. Lots of dreams about family and the parish and old friends, all good and full of a sense of peace. I had one where I saw my dad again, except he was younger like I had seen in pictures. He looked so good and happy. And Mom was there too. It was like they were at a picnic or something, except there were tons of people, and they were all looking up at the sky and laughing and pointing and gesturing to me; then I woke up. I don't know if that was from God or not, but it sure was a nice way to wake up amidst all that is going on.

After thinking through everything and praying some more, I think I see more clearly. I actually feel kinda bad for the government attorney and the whole government, for that matter. I get the commitment to peace, but at what cost? And what sort of peace will it be? I kinda feel like the older sibling who has to break the news to his little brother that there is no Santa Claus. I think that everybody has lost it and decided that they need to believe in a peace that is just a fairy tale. And sooner or later, the fairy tale will show itself for what it is. And so, I feel bad for these guys because they are giving their lives to this stuff and even willing to put people like me to death in order to keep believing in Santa Claus.

I suppose I should explain myself. I imagine lots of folks will think it is entirely the other way around. After all, the government's view is that all traditional religions are just shadows of the one true, humanistic religion made to preserve and advance mankind. And they base what they say on "the facts" as they see them. They say that the combination of science, an honest assessment of history, and the recent special guidance from "The Messengers" as they call themselves are proof enough of their positions.

Without immediately refuting their position, I want to lay out how I and the whole Church see it, as captured in the Encyclical of the Council on Church Unity.[9] Here it is in summary form:

- Truth is that which is and does not become untrue, both in its parts and its whole.[10,11]
- The sum of truth is self-evidentially beyond finite perception, and therefore finite means can never fully know it nor fully refute all untruth.[12]

---

[9] N.B. The whole Nicaean church, (East, West, South, North, Protestant, Catholic, Orthodox etc.) has experienced a reunion through its regular councils and its encyclicals under a common agreement on key doctrinal & functional issues including apostolic authority as captured in the scriptures, the nature and mission of the Church and its councils, a working agreement on cooperation etc.

[10] John 14:6, 15:26, Romans 1:25.

[11] Merriam-Webster's Online Dictionary, "truth", 2005

[12] "The LORD our God has secrets known to no one. We are not accountable for them, but we and our children are accountable forever for all that he

- Only God, the self-existent and eternal, infinite One can know truth wholly. We must assume his existence first before we begin to properly comprehend and apply truth.[13,14]

---

has revealed to us, so that we may obey all the terms of these instructions." (Deuteronomy 29:29)

"Oh, how great are God's riches and wisdom and knowledge! How impossible it is for us to understand his decisions and his ways! For who can know the LORD's thoughts? Who knows enough to give him advice? And who has given him so much that he needs to pay it back? For everything comes from him and exists by his power and is intended for his glory. All glory to him forever! Amen." (Romans 11:33–36)

"But God shows his anger from heaven against all sinful, wicked people who suppress the truth by their wickedness. They know the truth about God because he has made it obvious to them. For ever since the world was created, people have seen the earth and sky. Through everything God made, they can clearly see his invisible qualities – his eternal power and divine nature. So they have no excuse for not knowing God." (Romans 1:18–20)

For further reading see Nancy Pearcey, Total Truth: Liberating Christianity from Its Cultural Captivity, Copyright © 2004, 2005 by Nancy R. Pearcey Crossway Books, Wheaton, Illinois 60187 or John M. Frame, We Are All Philosophers: A Christian Introduction to Seven Fundamental Questions, Copyright 2019, Lexham Press, 1313 Commercial St., Bellingham, WA 98225

[13] Fear of the LORD is the foundation of true knowledge, but fools despise wisdom and discipline. (Proverbs 1:7)

[14] "But God shows his anger from heaven against all sinful, wicked people who suppress the truth by their wickedness. They know the truth about God because he has made it obvious to them. For ever since the world was created, people have seen the earth and sky. Through everything God made, they can clearly see his invisible qualities – his eternal power and

- God has revealed himself and the most necessary truth in His creation, through his word, and the revelation of Jesus Christ. [15,16,17]
- All truth begins with God, depends on God, and leads to God. [18]
- He is knowable yet beyond full knowledge. He is goodness, glory, and truth itself. [19]

---

divine nature. So they have no excuse for not knowing God. Yes, they knew God, but they wouldn't worship him as God or even give him thanks. And they began to think up foolish ideas of what God was like. As a result, their minds became dark and confused. Claiming to be wise, they instead became utter fools. And instead of worshiping the glorious, ever-living God, they worshiped idols made to look like mere people and birds and animals and reptiles. So God abandoned them to do whatever shameful things their hearts desired. As a result, they did vile and degrading things with each other's bodies. They traded the truth about God for a lie. So they worshiped and served the things God created instead of the Creator himself, who is worthy of eternal praise! Amen." (Romans 1:18-25)

[15] "[19] They know the truth about God because he has made it obvious to them. [20] For ever since the world was created, people have seen the earth and sky. Through everything God made, they can clearly see his invisible qualities – his eternal power and divine nature. So they have no excuse for not knowing God." (Romans 1:19–20)

[16] "Make them holy by your truth; teach them your word, which is truth." (John 17:17)

[17] "And you will know the truth, and the truth will set you free." (John 8:32)

[18] "For everything comes from him and exists by his power and is intended for his glory. All glory to him forever! Amen." (Romans 11:36)

[19] "Oh, how great are God's riches and wisdom and knowledge! How impossible it is for us to understand his decisions and his ways!" (Romans 11:33)

- Our highest good and glory is to know Him through his revealed truth and thus to live in his love, enjoy his glory, and serve him with all our being.[20,21,22]

Yeah, I know, pretty heady stuff. But it is really important to grasp because it is the basis for so much in this life. Concerning all that is going on with me, it is key. The government is asserting it knows the truth, but its sources are all finite and, therefore, necessarily will be limited and likely flawed. Even with the amazing recent revelation of "The Messengers" and their obvious supreme intellect, technology, and insight, they are still finite beings. Just because you have AI implants and commune with some sort of extra-terrestrials who have watched over the earth for eons and supposedly guided the development of humanity, you are not infallible nor infinite. (It also makes me really suspicious that "The Messengers" have been quick to deny that Jesus Christ has come in the flesh!)

---

[20] "Keep me safe, O God, for I have come to you for refuge. I said to the Lord, "You are my Master! Every good thing I have comes from you....You will show me the way of life, granting me the joy of your presence and the pleasures of living with you forever." (Psalm 16:1,2,11)

[21] "Always be full of joy in the Lord. I say it again—rejoice!" (Philippians 4:4)

[22] "I heard a loud shout from the throne, saying, "Look, God's home is now among his people! He will live with them, and they will be his people. God himself will be with them. He will wipe every tear from their eyes, and there will be no more death or sorrow or crying or pain. All these things are gone forever."" (Revelation 21:3–4)

8

Well, I've probably said enough for now. I hope the material from the encyclical makes sense. More to come tomorrow, Lord willing!

Thursday, August 11th

So, a little more on truth and all related stuff. I found early on in my life as a Christian that the object of all truth is God himself, the Trinity.[23] As cool as it is to stretch your brain to wrestle with the truth, whether as theology or philosophy or science, it is all meant to lead us to God himself. So, before I get into more of the details on truth, I want to dive into the deep end of the pool of truth, the Trinity.

We know God as Trinity through his revelation to us, especially through the word of God and the incarnation of Jesus Christ. We believe in the Trinity not because it all makes sense to us, but because God has revealed himself as such to us and called us to receive this truth and let it have its full effect.

I leave it to you to look up some of the verses. There are lots. But here are some for starters: Genesis 1:26, 3:22, 11:7, Deuteronomy 6:4-5. Psalm 45:6-7, Isaiah 9:6, 40:3, Matthew 3:16-17, 28:19, John 1;1-4, 14:26, 15:26,16:7,13-14, 17:20.28, Acts 5:3-4, Romans 9:5, 1 Corinthians 12:4-6, 2 Corinthians 13:14, Ephesians 4:4–6, 1 Peter 1:2, 1 John 2:1, Jude 20-21

Trinity is a word that combines Tri and Unity. It is just a concise way to say God is Three-In-One. This is the teaching of

---

[23] Please consider Michael Reeves, Delighting in the Trinity, IVP, Downers Grove, Illinois, 2012 for a very helpful and inspiring book on the Trinity.

scripture – that he is three persons, and yet he is one being. Both are taught clearly. That means that he is three persons in one being. As the old creed attributed to Athanasius says:

> "Whosoever will be saved, before all things, it is necessary that he hold the catholic faith. Which faith unless everyone does keep whole and undefiled, without doubt, he shall perish everlastingly. And the catholic faith is this: that we worship one God in Trinity, and Trinity in Unity; neither confounding the Persons nor dividing the Essence."[24]

And as the Council of 381 stated:

> "We believe in one God, the Father almighty, maker of heaven and earth, of all things visible and invisible. And in one Lord Jesus Christ, the only Son of God, begotten from the Father before all ages, God from God, Light from Light, true God from true God, begotten, not made; of the same essence as the Father.... And in the Holy Ghost, the Lord and Giver of life, who proceeds from the Father, who with the Father and the Son together is worshiped and glorified, who spoke by the prophets."[25]

So, why get into this mind-blowing stuff? Because this is who God is, and if we want to know what life is about, then we need to know what the author of life is like. And he has revealed

---

[24] Schaff, Philip (1877a), The Creeds of Christendom, 1, New York: Harper Brothers, OCLC 2589524,

[25] Philip Schaff, Creeds of Christendom, with a History and Critical Notes. Volume I. The History of Creeds. P27

himself to us as Trinity. And in knowing the Trinity, we truly know God, and there is not and cannot be anything greater.

What this means for me today is a few really helpful things. First, all that is, and all that will be is not an accident. It is not random. It is not chaotic. It all comes from a God who has existed in perfect union as three persons from eternity past into eternity future. And this creation flows out of this amazing eternal relationship between Father, Son, and Holy Spirit.[26] They created all things together with a plan in mind to share and show their great glory and goodness. And we get to be swept up in this great story they are working out.

Second, they have loved each other from eternity past and have loved us, their people, since before creation. And we are loved and swept up into the same intense and glorious divine love they have for one another. This is amazing that we are loved this much![27]

Third, Father[28], Son[29] , and Holy Spirit[30] are all working together to bring salvation to their people and redeem the entire cosmos.[31] This plan will be completed and is already well

---

[26] Read Genesis 1 with this in mind.

[27] See John 17:23, Ephesians 1:3-6 etc.

[28] See John 3:16, Ephesians 1:3-6, 1 Thessalonians 1:4, 1 Peter 1:3, 2:9 etc.

[29] See Isaiah 53:4-6, Romans 3:23-25, 1 Peter 1:3 etc.

[30] See Ezekiel 36:25-27, John 3:5-8, Titus 3:4-6 etc.

[31] See Colossians 1:19-20, 1 Corinthians 15:20-26

underway.[32] Setbacks and trials are part of the plan, but the conclusion is sure.[33] This plan of salvation and restoration is entirely a work of the Trinity. Salvation is of the Lord, alone.[34] It shows us the depths of God's goodness and glory. When adequately grasped and received, it generates sincere faith, life-giving hope and heart-felt love.[35]

So, knowing, experiencing, and loving God as Trinity is the engine that drives the train for all the other stuff. It works that way for me, especially lately. Don't get me wrong, it has been brutal thinking about losing so much. Even as I write this, my heart is broken. But I have something bigger than my heart, and He will get me through.

Friday, August 12th

Feeling pretty sick today. I know. Why am I sick when pretty much no one gets sick anymore? Well, in prison, you are quarantined and not given the immuno-boosters we all are so used to getting. As a result, getting sick is a real possibility. And this virus is hitting me hard. I think I know who gave it to me – there was a guy I was talking to during exercise break who looked kind of pale and sweaty. I must have got it from him.

---

[32] See Matthew 16:18, 25:14, 28:18-20 etc.

[33] See Acts 14:22, 1 Peter 4:12-13

[34] See John 6:44, 10:28-39, 14:6, Acts 4:12, Romans 3:21-26, 5:10, Ephesians 2:8, 1 Timothy 2:5-6, Titus 3:5

[35] See Romans 1:16, 1 Corinthians 15:3-4, 2 Corinthians 3:17-18, Galatians 5:5-6, Ephesians 1:15-23, 3:14-19, Colossians 1:3-5,

Even though I am nauseous, have a headache, and feel exhausted, I still was able to read my morning liturgy today. It has been so helpful to have the Book of Common Worship along with my Bible. I don't know what I'd do if they confiscated these. The Book of Common Worship is so helpful in guiding our daily life through various liturgies that shape us around biblical truth. This was one of the best things to come out of the reunification of the church and the yearly councils that meet. I think it was the Council on Church Unity that produced the Book of Common Worship and recommended using regular worship times throughout the day known as the "Offices."[36] Anyhow, here are some excerpts from the morning liturgy. This really lifted my spirit! Wish I had more, but this is about all I can write for now.

Hymn[37]

Come, O Creator Spirit, come,

And make within our hearts your home;

To us your grace eternal give,

Who of your breathing move and live.

Our senses with your light inflame,

Our hearts to heavenly love reclaim;

Our bodies' poor infirmity

---

[36] Consider: a) Justin Whitmel Earley, "The Common Rule," IVP, Downers Grove, Illinois, 2019, or b) Keller, Timothy J., Prayer: Experiencing Awe and Intimacy with God, Penguin Books, 2014, p. 240ff

[37] Universalis, Morning Prayer for Monday of week 20 in Ordinary Time, see https://universalis.com/lauds.htm

With strength perpetual fortify.
Our earthly foe afar repel:
    grant us henceforth in peace to dwell;
    and so to us, with you for guide,
    no ill shall come, no harm betide.
May we by you the Father learn,
And know the Son, and you discern,
Who are of both; and thus adore
In perfect faith for evermore.

Prayers and intercessions

Almighty Father, the heavens cannot hold your greatness:
    yet through your Son we have learned to say:
    – Father, may your Kingdom come!

We praise you as your children;
    may your name be kept holy in the hearts of all mankind.
    – Father, may your Kingdom come!

Help us to live in the hope of heaven today:
    make us ready to do your will on earth.
    – Father, may your Kingdom come!

Give us this day the courage to forgive others:
    as you forgive us our trespasses.
    – Father, may your Kingdom come!

Father, be with us in all our trials:
    do not allow us to fall away from you.
    – Father, may your Kingdom come!

Saturday, August 13th

Feeling much better. Oh boy, that was rough. They had to cart me down to the hospital after I passed out. The virus hit me hard – 40°C temp, chest pains, coughing, raging headache, bad nausea.

On top of being sick, I felt really low spiritually. It has been so very lonely at times being here. Even though I get to see Abby and the kids and some of our friends at least once a week, and even though I get to go outside every day for exercise and interaction with others, the isolation has worn me down. So, when I got really sick, it felt like I was falling apart. All the old idols I used to enjoy seemed to beckon me to satisfy myself in them. I could have easily run with them, at least in my mind. But as I cried out in prayer, two wonderful promises of Jesus came to me:

"For everyone has sinned; we all fall short of God's glorious standard. Yet God, in his grace, freely makes us right in his sight. He did this through Christ Jesus when he freed us from the penalty for our sins. For God presented Jesus as the sacrifice for sin. People are made right with God when they believe that Jesus sacrificed his life, shedding his blood."[38]

"All who love me will do what I say. My Father will love them, and we will come and make our home with each of them."[39]

---

[38] Romans 3:23–25a

[39] John 14:23

"Made right with God through the blood of Jesus – Jesus promising us to make our home with us," wow, those promises helped so much. And as I thought about it, I had a sense of God's nearness – a nearness you feel when you are at home with your loved ones around you. I knew in that moment that no matter how lonely I might feel, I am always forgiven, always accepted, always at home with him- all because of the free gift of Christ Jesus.

I not only experienced healing for my sick heart but also my sick body. I am so glad for the cures we discovered in the good days after the Cataclysm. And, so, so glad that when you are really sick here, they will actually use the medicine everyone else takes for granted. I am a new man today after the booster shot and the IV they game me. I don't want to see that again, if possible.

I am so glad that I got to be a small part of helping develop some of those cures. I loved my career as a Microbiologist. Although it was a ton of work to get through school, once I hit Grad school and got to do original research, it was all worth it. And the job I had at the old St. Luke's Medical Research Center in Boston was a dream job in a dream time. In some ways, I wish I could go back there right now and not have to deal with the mess we have today.

I am grateful for those good times, and I can trust God through these hard times.[40] I know who I have believed.[41] I

---

[40] See Future Grace, John Piper, Multnomah, 2005

[41] 2 Titus 1:12

know he is the real truth.[42] I know he is better than I can imagine.[43] I know he loves me and is for me.[44] I know he is in control.[45] And I know that I have something in him that will last forever when the memories of the good times and the hard times are thousands upon thousands of years behind us.[46] And this keeps me going![47]

Sunday, August 14th

The Lord's Day – no journaling today, just the morning worship liturgy, rest, time visiting with Abby (I can't wait!), and our daughter, Zoey, and her husband, Arman, and some good friends from our parish. Sundays are such a lifeline![48]

---

[42] John 14:6

[43] 1 Corinthians 2:9

[44] Romans 8:35-39

[45] Romans 8:28

[46] Revelation 21:4

[47] 1 Corinthians 15:58

[48] Psalm 122:1

Chapter 2: When I Was Young

Monday, August 15th

After all that heavy lifting, thinking about God and truth last week, I thought I'd make this week a little less stretching, thinking-wise. I want to share my story. I probably should have done that off the bat so you could know who this guy is who is sharing his "confessions," but better late than never!

I grew up in a loving home with a Hispanic mom and an Irish American dad. It made for interesting larger family gatherings, but all-in-all, both sides were a lot alike. They all valued family and celebrating together and a basic belief in God, though that only meant going to church for weddings, funerals, and Christmas. We had a lot of good times together.

I was the oldest, born in 2002 when my parents were in their early thirties. Mom grew up in town, where my Abuelito owned a large garment manufacturing company. Dad was one of the employees. They met at the factory when they were teenagers, moved in together after college, and got married in their late twenties. Then I came along.

I had the best of everything. Dad got promoted to management; Mom was one of the account reps for the company. We grew up in a really nice town, not too far from the factory. We had a big, beautiful home, a great yard, nice vacations, an excellent education, tons of friends, cool gaming systems, and lots of extra-curricular activities. Just about every night of the week and both days on the weekends were packed with sports and music lessons and Boy Scouts and stuff like that.[49]

Life was really good; the economy was booming, our family was relatively peaceful; we had tons of cousins and friends. What more could we ask?

Well, we could have asked for God, but we really didn't think we needed him. As a matter of fact, we found it very cringe when people talked about God. Belief in God was a personal thing, not something you should talk about in public. We thought that a secular approach to life was best for everybody. Faith was ok as long as it was kept private and personal. Politics, education, the workplace, and most social settings, and pretty much every-thing else around us seemed to reinforce that mindset.[50]

---

[49] In the West, the late 20th Century and early 21st Century was character-ized by busy, child-centered families, where the education and extra-curricular activities of the children in a family dominated the lifestyle of the family. This led to prioritizing the biological family to the exclusion of in-volvement with the local church. Consider a) Cameron Cole, "Busy All the Time: Over-Scheduled Children and the Freedom of the Gospel", The Gos-pel Coalition, January 12, 2014, b) Joseph Hellerman, "Our Priorities Are Off When Family Is More Important Than Church," Christianity Today, August 4, 2016, and c) Jamie Ivey, 3 Dangers of a Kid-Centered Family, ERLC, July 11, 2019.

[50] Lucas grew up with a secular worldview, whether he recognized it or not. This is just as much a religion as a Theistic worldview. Despite the myth that the secular view is somehow religiously neutral, it displays all the same qualities of any other religion/worldview. Also, sadly, it is too often exclu-sive, bigoted, intolerant and ignorant toward other worldviews, at least in

Tuesday, August 16th – When I was a sophomore in high school, I started to explore some ideas and lifestyles that previously were only things I had heard about from my friends and on social media. I had already had sex with my first girlfriend back in middle school. It wasn't a big deal to us at the time, given we had both been seeing nudity and pornography since grammar school and were brought up with pretty permissive values.[51]

But now, I started hooking up occasionally with female friends just for the fun of it. Then, I started to wonder if I was non-binary. We had been learning about that since middle school, and I had friends who identified that way. I had experienced some same-sex attraction and was wondering. Everyone said that if you are interested, then you should try it. So, like a lot of my peers, I explored. Our mindset was, "As long as it was safe and consensual, it was up to us." My exploration left me confused but leaning bisexual. So, I made that my label and went with it.[52]

---

the way it is practiced. For further reading see Nancy Pearcey, Chapters 1-4, Total Truth, CrossWay Books, 2005 or Smith, James K. A.. How (Not) to Be Secular, Wm. B. Eerdmans Publishing Co. for more discussion.

[51] The early 21st century secular Western mindset has trouble establishing a consistent sexual ethic that honors humans as bearers of God's image via their God-given sexuality.

[52] Gender dysphoria and sexual confusion are natural consequences of a corrupted understanding of what it means to be human (anthropology.) The scriptures give us a solid basis to understand our humanity and thus our gender identity and sexual orientation.

It wasn't that I was having sex regularly. But I definitely was not abstaining when I had the opportunity. Threesomes were becoming popular back then.[53] After trying it once, I knew they were not for me. I had some limits when it came to sex.

But sex wasn't the only area of exploration for me. Some of my friends were getting hooked on heroin. That scared me too much. But marijuana was legal and seemed safe and good for chillaxing with my friends, as we used to say. So, I started smoking pot pretty regularly. I experimented with cocaine but was kind of scared of that too. Alcohol was something that was always around my family at parties, most drank responsibly, so I was used to that and was more or less only a social drinker keeping my limit to the weekends and three drinks a night.[54]

I don't share all this for your entertainment, but so you would understand how I saw life at the time. And I was very typical of my peers. Our biggest values were tolerance, authenticity, loyalty to our friends, and avoiding offending or hurting someone. Beyond that, we didn't believe in that many absolutes. We thought the road forward was best without traditional values on sex, religion, and conservative politics.

Traditional values seemed to be part of all the hypocrisy of the religious right and baby boomer curmudgeons that were

---

[53] Confusion on gender and sexual identity would naturally lead to alternative sexual behavior previously considered unnatural. This is the natural progression of rejecting the counsel of God. See Romans 1:18-32.

[54] Substance abuse is also a natural outcome of failure to find in God the satisfaction, strength, comfort and joy needed for life. See Psalm 4:7, 16:11, Jeremiah 2:11-13, Ephesians 5:18, Revelation 21-22.

just power-hungry in our opinion. We wanted real values – like equality, justice, peace, and understanding. And we thought the best way to get there was to tear down the old ways and find a better way. Little did we know, this approach did a lot of harm to many of the good things we had in our imperfect world.

Wednesday, August 17th

My senior year in high school was the year when the coronavirus pandemic hit the world. Our world was filled with quarantining, social distancing, masks, and lots of bad news about elderly relatives and friends dying. School was canceled and then went online, if you can call it school. I had an online graduation with a car parade for a party.

I went off to college as a freshman at Cornell in mid-August and was home by Thanksgiving. Two-thirds of all classes were online, from my dorm room. The other third was in person, socially distanced with a mask. We got close to the other nine people in our student cohort. But other than that, no sports, no parties, just lame school-sponsored events with social distancing from people outside your cohort.

Before Thanksgiving, there was an election. That election was the start of a series of events that released a giant dam full of hate and rage that was already about to burst. And burst it did. Although the pandemic declined and we got a working vaccine by the end of 2021, the protests, riots, violence and global instability got worse and worse. It was a wonder that I was able to last through my remaining years of college. I was right in the thick of it, along with all my friends.

Two friends of mine and I got involved with an anarchist group.[55] It wasn't because we wanted true anarchy but because we considered the current hierarchy to be racist, corrupt, unjust, and power-hungry. We believed the only way to change things was to unseat them entirely. So, I gave much of my free time to showing up at protests and doing my best to confront racists and vandalize the bourgeoisie, at least as I saw them. I look back now and see that my life was defined by the same mindset of the ancient Greek cynics and skeptics.[56] There is nothing new under the sun![57]

Thursday, August 18th

Despite so much time given to protests and my political activities, I was able to do fairly well in college and get into MIT for grad school. It was good to be a little closer to home. It also marked a transition in my life in terms of faith. Finishing undergrad and starting at MIT got me thinking about what I wanted my life to look like. And that got me thinking about

---

[55] Anarchists are those who wish to overthrow the current authority structures. They may do so for various reasons ranging across the political spectrum. They may differ on the final form of authority structures but would tend toward minimizing authority structures. See https://wikipedia.org/wiki/Anarchism for a good discussion of this.

[56] Lucas' commitments were a fresh recycling of the views and outcomes of the ancient Greek Skeptics and Cynics. These views have been influential through the ages. Consider Descartes and Nietzsche, among others. If you deconstruct everything you are left with nothing. Contrast this with receiving divine revelation as the basis for further understanding and practice. See Proverbs 1:7 etc.

[57] Ecclesiastes 1:9

what would really make me happy. And that got me wondering if anything could really make me happy. And that made me really sad. I started thinking through the things that brought me the greatest pleasure in life – hanging with good friends, my family, snowboarding, parties, sex, causing a ruckus at protests – and I felt like all of them could never give me what I needed. That was when I met Ryan.

Ryan was a fellow grad student. He was from metro Boston, too, and came from a close-knit extended family like me. But he was different. I actually met him because I thought he might be interested in guys – kinda embarrassing now. Ryan was nice, thanked me for the compliment, and told me that he was saving sex for marriage to a woman. That shocked me and almost made me laugh out loud right there in front of him. He asked me if I would be willing to go to lunch and talk about it. Wow. What a right reply at the right time!

Over lunch, Ryan told me about his faith and how God gave us sex to reflect the love, intimacy, and joy of the Trinity. He told me it was meant to be a real experience but ultimately to point to the ultimate real thing. The ultimate real thing was intimately knowing and experiencing God. And so God designed sex to point to what knowing him is like, and in this life, it does that through a monogamous, life-long marriage between a man and a woman in their God-given complementary designs.[58]

---

[58] See Karol Józef Wojtyła, Theology of the Body, Rome, 1997 or its introduction: Christopher West, Theology of the Body for Beginners: A Basic Introduction to Pope John Paul II's Sexual Revolution (West Chester, PA:

The last part I had heard before, but the first idea was mind-blowing for me. I had a ton of questions. I tried my best to be respectful, but I know Ryan winced a few times as I ask loaded questions that pretty clearly implied he was ignorant. But he kept on listening and asking me questions and patiently explaining the Christian faith.

That first lunch with Ryan was the beginning of hours and hours of conversations with him and some of his other friends at church who became my friends too. I got involved with the young adult group at his church and found some of the best friends I had ever known.

One of the things that was most compelling was how Christianity explained the human experience in terms of creation, fall, and redemption. It explained why & how everything exists, how things got messed up, and how God is redeeming and renewing all things. I realized that this pattern is more or less followed for all philosophies of life, consciously or not, explicitly "religious" or "secular," so-called. It is just a question of which one is true and therefore truly works.

Just for a moment, consider the common western secular philosophy. The creation story is that we are all products of a materialist universe, subject to certain laws that have shaped us into the highly evolved material beings we are. The fall story is that this universe has mutations, defects, and anomalies, as well as human agents who can choose to act helpfully or not. As a

---

Ascension, 2004). Another resource in this line: Nancy R. Pearcey, Love Thy Body: Answering Hard Questions about Life and Sexuality (Grand Rapids, MI: Baker, 2018).

result, seemingly bad things happen to good people. The redemption story is that through good science, common sense, and mutually beneficial cooperation, we can build a better future together. There you have it, creation, fall, and redemption. Hope that example helps!

Anyhow, as I talked with my new friends and wrestled through so many topics, it seemed like I was finding some real, solid ground to stand on. All this, while the world around us seemed to be shaking and falling with no more solid ground. The collapse of the West as we knew it was beginning. This historic solid ground that so many had relied on was disappearing even as so many like me found new ground to stand on in the historic Christian faith.

Friday, August 19th

It probably would be good to explain how my friendship with Ryan and my journey towards Christianity addressed my values on the hot topics of my day: sex, gender, politics, and faith.

As you know from reading, my perspective was pretty different than a Christian perspective, at least on most fronts. I also had a lot of prejudice and misunderstanding when it came to Christianity. It seemed to me to be more about old-fashioned values and Republican party politics. I assumed religious people were less educated, anti-science, and anti-progressive.[59] Ryan and his church showed me otherwise in unexpected ways.

First, I quickly found out that Ryan, his family, and his friends were all pretty bright and fairly well-educated. Ryan's dad had a Doctorate in science and a Master's in biblical languages. His mom was the smartest person I've ever met, giving up a lucrative research chair at the Jonas Salk Institute so she could raise a family and support her husband's career. She was a popular part-time professor at MIT in Biological Physics.

Second, they were anything but "narrow-minded conservatives."[60] They didn't align with any one party but followed a political philosophy that eventually was refined and expressed by the Council on Church & State. It defined the government (in formal speak – the "state") as one of the many parallel spheres of authority among humankind that has a legitimate but limited function alongside other important equally-authoritative spheres such as family, church, education, agriculture, science, and the arts.[61] As a result, they didn't look to the state

---

[59] See, for example, U.S. Adults See Evangelicals Through a Political Lens, Barna, November 21, 2019.

[60] Consider Amy E. Black (Editor), Stanley N. Gundry (Editor), Five Views on the Church and Politics, Zondervan, 2015

[61] "In a Calvinistic sense we understand hereby, that the family, the business, science, art and so forth are all social spheres, which do not owe their existence to the state, and which do not derive the law of their life from the superiority of the state, but obey a high authority within their own bosom; an authority which rules, by the grace of God, just as the sovereignty of the State does." Kuyper, Abraham. Lectures on Calvinism (p. 90). Eerdmans Publishing Co., Grand Rapids, 1931

to do what the other spheres should do. They also were very supportive of appropriate efforts by the state to act within its sphere and empower the other spheres, including issues formerly championed by the left and the right. This didn't fit under anything I had known. [62]

Furthermore, they supported the church and other spheres speaking independently and extensively to issues like immigration, care of the poor, respect for the marginalized, right to life, ethics, economics, business practices and whatever else needed to be addressed. I found this all so very different and, in many ways, very refreshing. It challenged my belief that the key to everything was the state. I had subscribed to the idea that the state controls all and whoever controls the state controls all. This new teaching was very different than my view. It was conservative but also very progressive. It caused me to reassess all my previous categories.

Regarding sex and gender, that was even more radical. I was committed to gender fluidity and responsible but free sex. Then Ryan and his buddies introduced God into the equation. I scoffed at first. But the more I heard, the more I read, the more I pondered, and, surprisingly, the more I prayed, the more I started to see things differently.

First, I had to see that another view was feasible, not just another view on gender and sex but another view on how we determine truth. Then, I had to see that another view actually

[62] Consider Stephen V. Monsma, J. Christopher Soper, The Challenge of Pluralism: Church and State in Five Democracies, Rowman & Littlefield, 1997

made good sense. Oh, how I hated to admit this at first! Then, over time, probably the hardest thing was to see that another view was actually preferable.

This all took a little while but happened to me in the context of my friends in my church. There were lots of things that led me through this process: our many late-night discussions, our very honest sharing of struggles, our prayer together, our discussions of good books like "engendered" by Sam Andreades, and poems like "A Valediction: Forbidding Mourning" by John Donne, along with lots of time with married couples in our church who were learning to live these things out in the ups and downs of normal life.

It wasn't until I got to the final point where I saw the Christian view as not only true but good and not only good but incredibly beautiful that I finally found the ability to leave behind my bisexuality and hook-up lifestyle.[63] And when I did that, I was finally free to embrace Jesus as my rescuer and my King.[64] Previously, I was blind to my sin and ignorance, but now, in light of his truth, goodness, and glory, I saw things as they really are. So, I ran to King Jesus and embraced him as the atonement for my sins and the fountain of true life for my body and soul. And I started a life-long journey of learning to follow him.

---

[63] Romans 12:2

[64] Consider Thomas Chalmers, The Expulsive Power of a New Affection, Crossway, 2020

Saturday, August 20th

That milestone happened somewhere during the first semester of my second year of grad school. I was baptized that winter, indoors, of course! That was after probably 1,000 hours of arguing and asking and listening on just about every item we could debate, including who was the best quarterback of all time (still not sure of that one.)

I am so grateful for my friend Ryan and everyone else at what is now East Cambridge Parish Church of the Trinity. They remain like our family. I can't believe they actually had the patience and the love to endure with me all that time. I truly saw Jesus through them. And once I truly saw him, I could never leave him.

I experienced a new life back in grad school. I came to understand who Jesus really is and what it means to trust him and follow him. It happened because when I was hurting and confused, someone loved me like Jesus. They loved me by listening to me, not judging me, being patient, answering my questions, accepting me like family, not being intimidated by me, and praying a ton for me. I got to see and feel what it was like to believe and follow Jesus before I actually did.[65] So, once I made the decision, it made all the sense in the world.

I know now that all the while, often in undetected ways, often in tangible ways, God was working to draw me to himself. And that work was motivated by an eternal, measureless ocean

---

[65] See Tim Keller, Center Church, Zondervan, Grand Rapids, Michigan, 2012, "Missional Evangelism through Mini-Decisions" pp. 281–82.

of love for an undeserving sinner like me. I am so glad that Jesus suffered and died on that cross for me so that I get to live a new life in him. Early on, Galatians 2:20 became a favorite verse; it has motivated and protected me through so many trials, temptations, and challenges. I hope it helps you too.

"My old self has been crucified with Christ. It is no longer I who live, but Christ lives in me. So I live in this earthly body by trusting in the Son of God, who loved me and gave himself for me."[66]

Sunday, August 21st

No journaling today. I get to see Abby again and our oldest grandchild, who is taking this really hard. I pray God visits us as we visit together. Here is an excerpt from the liturgy from the Book of Common Worship I am praying for today. Praying out of this liturgy has helped me so many times in my life as I have struggled with dashed hopes and dreams. I hope it helps you.

Death of a Dream:

O Christ, in whom the final fulfillment of all hope is held secure.

I bring to you now the weathered fragments of my former dreams, the broken pieces of my expectations, the rent patches of hopes worn thin, the shards of some shattered image of life as I once thought it would be.

---

[66] Galatians 2:20

What I so wanted has not come to pass. I invested my hopes in desires that returned only sorrow and frustration. Those dreams, like glimmering faerie feasts, could not sustain me, and in my head, I know that you are sovereign even over this – over my tears, my confusion, and my disappointment. But I still feel, in this moment, as if I have been abandoned, as if you do not care that these hopes have collapsed to rubble.

And yet I know this is not so. You are the sovereign of my sorrow. You apprehend a wider sweep with wiser eyes than mine. My history bears the fingerprints of grace. You were always faithful, though I could not always trace quick evidence of your presence in my pain, yet did you remain at work, lurking in the wings, sifting all my splinterings for bright embers that might be breathed into more eternal dreams.

Not my dreams. O Lord, not my dreams, but yours, be done. Amen. [67]

---

[67] A Liturgy for the Death of a Dream, Douglas McKelvey, Every Moment Holy, Rabbit Room Press (2017)

Chapter 3: Dreams Come True

Monday, August 22nd

I mentioned broken dreams in Sunday's post. I know it feels like we are living through a broken dream right now, but my life has already been so full of fulfilled dreams. Soon after finding new life in Christ when I never expected it, I found new life with the woman of my dreams. Abby was part of the local parish that was so instrumental in my faith journey. The first time I met her, I was interested in her. Little did I know that within 15 months, we would end up getting married.

Abby had grown up in church but rebelled when she left home. Her experience was probably not too different from mine in terms of lifestyle choices and perspectives. Even though she had a background in the Christian faith, it hadn't gripped her mind and heart in a way that held her. She saw it more in terms of rule-keeping and self-denial instead of knowing, loving, and experience the best that could possibly be. So, when better options came her way, she left her upbringing behind to finally find things she really enjoyed – at least that's what she thought.

After dropping out of art school, she had a pretty successful stint as a lead singer in a vocal trance band along with lots of drugs, alcohol, parties, and sex. But no one can keep that up too long. After two years of pretty wild living, Abby hit a wall, literally. While driving on the highway, she blacked out from some bad drugs and was almost killed when she crashed into a highway noise barrier. She was in ICU for two weeks. When she finally got out of the hospital, she checked herself into a rehab center to get clean and somehow to find a way forward. During that time, someone gave her a book called "The Prodigal God" by the old theologian Tim Keller.[68] She saw herself in that story and felt God himself speak to her and call her home. It was pretty dramatic. When she finished her rehab program, she made her way back to the Boston area, got a job, finished school, got baptized, and joined a good church. She has never looked back and continues to use her unusual musical and artistic gifts to touch many lives.

We started dating a month after I was baptized. It was a pretty intense ten months of falling head over heels for each other. We got married in January of my third year of grad school, had our first child a couple of years after that, with three more, and two miscarriages to follow. We've had our challenges but have grown to love and enjoy each other more and more as we have gone through life. She is my dream woman.

Tuesday, August 23rd

Another dream for me was being able to work as a research scientist in microbiology. I finished my Ph.D. at MIT in four years. By that time, the influence of the church in science was growing dramatically. After the many waves of political crises of the early 21st century and the Cataclysm when most of the West fell to anarchy and military coups, the church woke up and started cooperating unlike any time since the Apostles. Part of

---

[68] Keller, T. (2011). The Prodigal God: Recovering the Heart of the Christian Faith (Reprint ed.). Penguin Books.

that cooperation was concerted efforts to understand and promote a Christian view of the sciences. The old idea that the best science was secular science was being replaced by a greater honesty about the presuppositions inherent in the scientific endeavor. As a result, many more young people were pursuing the sciences with a sense of call from God to explore, learn, and serve mankind. I got to be a part of that.

My new career fit hand-in-glove with my new faith. It made what might have otherwise been tedious into something that often felt like a romantic adventure. I know that sounds kinda dramatic, but being able to probe all the intricacies of God's good creation with a sense that I was helping to fulfill his plan for humankind inspired me. The biblical call to steward creation as those reflecting his creative genius was right there at the beginning of the story. And I got to be part of that story through my vocation in science.

My lab had been formed by a bunch of Christian biotech researchers and venture capitalists who wanted to create a dream team to solve some of the greatest challenges in healthcare. My team was tasked with studying viruses and working towards some sort of broad-spectrum treatment, if possible.

Our work on fungal extracts led to the first broad-spectrum anti-viral vaccine. It was such a privilege to be part of that team and see, after thousands of hours of research, lots of prayer and brainstorming, and lots of help from other labs, something that really made a difference in the world. As a result of our work, not only was there a cure for the common cold (most of them), but also a dramatic reduction in viral-induced cancers like bone, brain, cervical, liver, and lung cancers and various lymphomas. As I write this, I am overwhelmed with emotion. Being a part of that sort of research was like living in a dream you never wanted to end. Sorry, but I can't help but feel this way about that time in my life.

Wednesday, August 24th

It probably would be good to address how I understood evolutionary theory as a Christian microbiologist. I believe Charles Darwin did a lot of good in his work and a lot of evil, unwittingly. The good he did was to ask bold questions and posit bold answers that forced us to better examine the biological world around us. The evil he did was to not adequately address the limitations of the scientific method and the temptations of overconfident theorizing. Not that it was his responsibility to police all future scientific endeavors, but his theory led the way in a less-than-humble scientific ethos that, ironically, ended up stunting scientific progress.

True science involves using instrumentation that characterizes the physical aspects of our world to investigate phenomena. This is followed by formulating a hypothesis, testing and confirming that hypothesis, and then, if consistently confirmed over a long period of time, characterizing that hypothesis as a fact of science. Short of these steps, it really isn't science but something else. Something we can call "Scientism".[69] Too often, these steps were neglected, and those who questioned unproven theories were ostracized from the scientific community.

---

[69] Consider https://en.wikipedia.org/wiki/Scientism

This is what happened to those who proposed intelligent design in the area of evolutionary science.[70] They were treated with great bigotry and scientific hypocrisy. The followers of Scientism failed to see that their assumptions that a very ancient universe miraculously produced incredible complexity was a great leap of faith. This complexity is so statistically impossible that belief in it exceeds the faith needed to believe that the universe was formed with a specific design to support life, ultimately human life, on planet earth. Their commitment to the presupposition of a materialistic universe created circular logic in their scientific inquiries that blinded them to other viable explanations and, ironically, stunted the progress of science. If you are really going to practice good science, you must be open to all hypotheses, not just the hypotheses that confirm your previous commitments.

I hold to a view of evolution that is common among many Christians and endorsed by the Council on Science and Faith. I believe that the universe was created by God out of nothing and brought into being to display his glory. I believe that humankind was specially and intentionally created by God in his image to reflect what he is like as the pinnacle of creation. I believe that the universe follows many laws, known and unknown, established by God to bring order and prosperity to the universe. I believe that our understanding of exactly how he has done this is necessarily limited.

---

[70] Nancy Pearcey, Total Truth (Study Guide Edition – Trade Paperback) (p. 168). Crossway. Kindle Edition.

Though it is fitting for us to investigate and postulate how things came to be, we cannot be sure, especially when we are looking far beyond our current time, either into the past or into the future. Things can appear to have been formed through a certain process when they aren't. God has established rules for his universe, but he is not governed by them. If he can create the miracle we call the universe, then he can create other miracles that don't seem to fit in our universe. Just as he turned water into wine and walked on water, he can do anything he pleases. So, in regard to evolutionary biology, we should investigate and hypothesize based on what we know but always be prepared for a different mechanism than the one that seems most likely. I am very comfortable with this level of mystery because it is inherent in the nature of a supreme being and evident in the vastness of our universe.

I think that a very old creation fits with much of what we observe. I think that progress from simple to complex organisms is seen to a degree in the fossil record, in genetics, in biology, in the species, and in other observations. But, even so, there are many gaps and serious deficiencies with a naturalistic evolutionary view.[71] So, I am content with a view that we can call a chastened theistic evolutionary model. It is chastened because I am fully ready to be told the wine was water an instant before

[71] Consult a) Stephen C. Meyer, Darwin's Doubt, Harper Collins, New York, NY, 2014, b) Phillip E. Johnson, Darwin on Trial (Downers Grove, Ill.: InterVarsity Press, 1993), c) Michael Behe, Darwin's Black Box: The Biochemical Challenge to Evolution (New York: Touchstone, 1996), or d) The Creation Hypothesis: Scientific Evidence for an Intelligent Designer, ed. J. P. Moreland (Downers Grove, Ill.: InterVarsity: 1994);

I drank it. It is theistic because intelligent design is so obvious and necessary. It is evolutionary because we can see progress from simple to complex. This view does not demand I subscribe to any gradual transition from one species to another. I find this very unlikely, given the symbiotic nature of biological systems, the lack of fossil evidence, and the most apparent reading of scripture that teaches us God made each species distinctly.[72]

I hope that makes sense and presents something you can work with. It isn't merely my personal view, but the view held by many Christians in science and endorsed by the Council on Science and Faith, as I mentioned. You can read more about this in their lengthy statement on faith and science. It was a major breakthrough in many ways, and I am grateful for the tremendous help it gave in the progress of science and faith. I'll write more tomorrow.

Thursday, August 25th

Well, what about people? How do we understand them, as far as science and faith go? That is a really important question. I've already said a lot on this topic, but I think it would be important to put it all together.

When I was young, the prevalent perspectives on what it means to be human were radically different than the biblical perspective. The current perspectives that have appeared with "The Messengers" are more of the same. Let me briefly talk about a few of them as I see them.

---

[72] Genesis 1:12, 21.

First, there is the secular sociological perspective, which says that man is a social animal that forms social units and social structures for the mutual survival of the species. These social units are derived from various impulses built into the biology of humanity. However, in this model, the focus is on the social side of humans. Humans form social structures to advance the interests of the group. These structures are about the exercise of power – power to preserve the group and power to resist or oppress those outside the group. The metanarratives, norms, ethos, and lifestyle of the group revolve around the advancement of the group through the exercise of power. Social groups will compete with each other, and the most powerful group will win. However, society as a whole will most benefit itself if it allows and advances the maximum diversity of social structures. So, to move forward, humankind, the social animal, must learn to tolerate and coexist as each group respectively seeks to survive and thrive.

Second, there is the man-as-biology perspective. This is related to other theories but emphasizes humankind as simply biology in motion. Our genetics and our biological functions determine everything about us, for good or for bad. Even our sense of art and philosophy, ethics, and religion are products of a long process of evolutionary biology that produced humanity. Everything about us is merely for the purpose of the survival and propagation of the human species. All our problems are rooted in biology, either in helpful or unhelpful genetic traits.

Third, there is the man-as-the-choice maker perspective. This is related to the previous two but deserves its own discussion. This view says you are the product of the choices you make. And those choices don't necessarily have any meaning other than the meaning you assign them. Nobody can present undeniable truth to prove conclusively that you are wrong in your choice. Therefore, you must be the one to choose and decide what and who you will be. All the norms handed to us from society are ultimately random as well, so we should feel free to recreate our own norms, as long as they don't bring harm to others.

As you can see, this is all somewhat self-defeating – how do we define harm in the first place? How do we make the choice that choices can be freely made? Nevertheless, choose away. If you want to be of a different gender, you can do so. If you want to see yourself as the world's greatest artist, why not? If you want to go live in a commune where you share everything in common, that is up to you. To be human is to choose.

There are other ideas out there as well. Like I said, they have made a comeback recently. But you will find a lot in common with these three ideas. With that background set, tomorrow, I will present the biblical view of humanity.

Friday, August 26th

Thanks for bearing with me on this current subject. It may seem kinda academic, but it is so important and something that affects us whether we know it or not.

The biblical view of humanity is at its core the view that we are made as the image of God. This phrase is used in the beginning of the Bible when God creates humankind.

"Then God said, "Let us make human beings in our image, to be like us. They will reign over the fish in the sea, the birds in the sky, the livestock, all the wild animals on the earth, and the small animals that scurry along the ground." So God created human beings in his own image. In the image of God he created them; male and female he created them. Then God blessed them and said, "Be fruitful and multiply. Fill the earth and govern it. Reign over the fish in the sea, the birds in the sky, and all the animals that scurry along the ground."[73]

Without getting into everything that is here, let me point out four things we learn from this. 1) God says, "let us... in our image," it is a plurality that we image. 2) We are the image of God – we reflect him. 3) We are made male and female; we reflect his image as a binary in community. 4) We carry out this image as we are fruitful, multiply, and reign over creation.

So, we are made to be like God to reflect who he is. That is the meaning of being his image. We are necessarily, therefore, relational and communal, for God is an "us." We are a complimentary binary as male and female who together image God. We are to fill the earth with this image and reign over creation as part of the task of imaging God.

This understanding has far-ranging implications. We have tremendous dignity as being made in the image of God himself. We are made to be in relationship with each other. We are designed with a specific gender that is necessary as part of our humanity. We are created but also stand over the rest of creation, not under it. We are to be prosperous and advance our call

---

[73] Genesis 1:26-28

to image God. These mandates are so very important in having a healthy view of mankind. I submit that they far exceed anything the alternate perspectives offer.

This all sounds great. But what went wrong? Well, I'll cover the rest of the story briefly tomorrow.

Saturday, August 27th

I think the best way to cover the rest of the story is to spring off of what it says in 1 Corinthians 15:21-26.

> *"So you see, just as death came into the world through a man, now the resurrection from the dead has begun through another man. Just as everyone dies because we all belong to Adam, everyone who belongs to Christ will be given new life. But there is an order to this resurrection: Christ was raised as the first of the harvest; then all who belong to Christ will be raised when he comes back. After that the end will come, when he will turn the Kingdom over to God the Father, having destroyed every ruler and authority and power. For Christ must reign until he humbles all his enemies beneath his feet. And the last enemy to be destroyed is death."*

The original man, Adam, fell into sin and rebellion against his Creator, along with his wife, Eve. And they plunged all their descendants into the same consequences they experienced, death, spiritual and then physical. We call this 'the fall'. And it has marred humanity and creation ever since. As good as creation is, it has existed in a fallen state since that initial fall. As a result, everything is tainted by sin and brokenness.

But God has not given up. He has entered into creation as a man, the second Adam, so to speak.[74] God in the flesh, Jesus of Nazareth, came as the perfect man, died in our stead the death we deserve for our sin and rebellion, and rose again on the third day, victorious over sin and death. And all who belong to him, through simple faith in him, receive a spiritual and eventually a physical resurrection. The resurrected Jesus now reigns to put all his enemies under his feet, and once that is done, he will finally destroy that last and terrible enemy, death.[75] This is the redemption that God is working in his creation.

So, if we are to understand humankind, we must understand ourselves through the storyline of creation, fall, and redemption. When we see ourselves as made in the image of God, fallen and marred by sin but redeemed for the true fulfillment of our created purposes, we will see ourselves as God sees us and live the life he has called us to live.

I hope this makes sense. Even more importantly, I hope it fills your mind, heart, and body with joy and hope and purpose. We are amazing creations, unlike any others. We are loved by God and called to something truly amazing. And we get to

---

[74] Consider Romans 5:17: "For the sin of this one man, Adam, caused death to rule over many. But even greater is God's wonderful grace and his gift of righteousness, for all who receive it will live in triumph over sin and death through this one man, Jesus Christ."

[75] As in 1 Corinthians 15:25–26 :"For Christ must reign until he humbles all his enemies beneath his feet. And the last enemy to be destroyed is death."

experience this in all we do, including how we worship as his people on Sundays. That's next.

Sunday, August 28th

As I have said, I try not to journal on Sundays but instead focus on worship, visiting with family and friends, and resting. I hope this Sunday commitment makes more sense in light of all we talked about this week. I am excited for my time today. I am planning to get with Abby and my youngest son this week. It will be sweet to catch up, read scripture, pray, and celebrate our Sunday liturgy. This is the song I have planned for our time, it's an old one but literally one of the best for what we have been looking at this week. I'll leave you with that for now.

How Great Thou Art[76]

Verse 1

> O Lord my God
> When I in awesome wonder
> Consider all the worlds
> Thy hands have made
> I see the stars
> I hear the rolling thunder
> Thy pow'r thru'out
> The universe displayed

---

[76] CCLI Song # 14181, Stuart Wesley Keene Hine, © Copyright 1949 and 1953 Stuart Hine Trust CIO Stuart K. Hine Trust, CCLI License # 11098836

> Then sings my soul
> My Savior God to Thee
> How great Thou art
> How great Thou art
> Then sings my soul
> My Savior God to Thee
> How great Thou art
> How great Thou art

Verse 2

> When through the woods
> And forest glades I wander
> And hear the birds
> Sing sweetly in the trees
> When I look down
> From lofty mountain grandeur
> And hear the brook
> And feel the gentle breeze

Verse 3

> And when I think
> That God His Son not sparing
> Sent Him to die
> I scarce can take it in
> That on the cross
> My burden gladly bearing
> He bled and died
> To take away my sin

Verse 4

When Christ shall come
With shout of acclamation
And take me home
What joy shall fill my heart
Then I shall bow
In humble adoration
And there proclaim
My God how great Thou art

Chapter 4: Jesus is Lord, not Caesar

Monday, August 29th

I had a meeting with the lawyer for the government and my lawyer this morning. I had to update them on my response to the sentencing. Before he invited me to reply, he said, "I really hope you have decided not to be so radical about all this and spare everybody, including your loved ones, the pain of going through with this." That was quite an introduction. I believe he truly wants to spare us pain, but the only course he is allowing is the one he picks. And that course labels all who do not follow the government's view of life as radicals. While I believe people can be too radical about things, merely having a difference and being consistent with that difference is not being radical. I am simply looking to follow Christ and live a relatively quiet Christian life submitting to authorities as best as I can, as long as it doesn't involve disobeying God.

But to be silent about the truth, about my faith, about a way of life that has brought tremendous temporal and eternal good to billions of precious people, is a most unloving and even cowardly betrayal of all that is good and right and glorious. I told him this. His face got all contorted with anger and frustration. I think I understand. But I also don't understand, for he and I hold a radically different view of not only what it means to be human but also how the government is meant to function in life. That is what I think I should write about this week – the government or "state" as it is called by the academics. It is oh so important to have a biblical view of politics and government. I hope I can help with my reflections on this. I have already mentioned a good bit, but I will use this week to get into a little more.

Let me introduce a key passage of scripture on this and then get into more stuff in the following days. Here it is, Matthew 22:15-22.

> *"Then the Pharisees met together to plot how to trap Jesus into saying something for which he could be arrested. They sent some of their disciples, along with the supporters of Herod, to meet with him. "Teacher," they said, "we know how honest you are. You teach the way of God truthfully. You are impartial and don't play favorites. Now tell us what you think about this: Is it right to pay taxes to Caesar or not?" But Jesus knew their evil motives. "You hypocrites!" he said. "Why are you trying to trap me? Here, show me the coin used for the tax." When they handed him a Roman coin, he asked, "Whose picture and title are stamped on it?" "Caesar's," they replied. "Well, then," he said, "give to Caesar what belongs to Caesar, and give to God what belongs to God." His reply amazed them, and they went away."*

Two groups who had very different views of the Roman government got together to trap Jesus. The Pharisees rejected the Roman government and supported returning to a theocracy under a monarch according to previous Israeli history. The Herodians supported the Roman government as legitimate in every way. The Pharisees and Herodians were normally enemies but, "the enemy of my enemy is my friend," as they say. So, it was here.

They thought they could trap Jesus between them, either getting him in trouble with those who supported the Roman

52

government or with those who rejected the Roman government and supported a theocracy. There seemed no way out of this one. But they didn't know Jesus very well.

He asked for the coin that was used to pay taxes and had them tell them who's image was on the coin. He then gave his succinct and profound reply, "give to Caesar what belongs to Caesar, and give to God what belongs to God."

He both legitimized non-theocratic human government and limited its scope. Of course, everything belongs to God, so God's sphere is not limited. And God presides over all the spheres he has ordained for the thriving of humanity – the family, the church, the marketplace, education, and the local, regional, and national governments. Jesus is teaching that Caesar's sphere, as the highest state authority, is both legitimate but limited and not synonymous with God's sphere.

This was radically different from the prevailing notion, then and now, that the rule of government was all-encompassing. That was why this was such a controversial question for Jesus to answer. The Romans had to proclaim that "Caesar is Lord." Yet, this teaching said otherwise. The Pharisees insisted that government must be theocracy under the Old Covenant. This teach said government is legitimate even when a "Caesar" ran it. Jesus radically adjusted our understanding of the role of human government in this current age, an age between the legitimate theocratic government of ancient Israel and the legitimate theocratic government of Jesus' final kingdom. Human government is legitimate but limited. It occupies a sphere under God alongside any other sphere God deems legitimate.

Caesar isn't Lord, but he does have a role to play, and that role is sanctioned by God.

So, what my lawyer friend thinks and does is a contradiction to what Jesus taught. Government is the ultimate authority for him and is meant to hold sway over even the convictions of our hearts and the words we speak. There is no room for another authority, ultimately, in his philosophy. This has been, more or less, the expectation of so many for so many hundreds of years. Thankfully, we had almost 50 years of a different view, at least until recently.

Tuesday, August 30th

Sorry if this stuff on government is boring. I am covering it because it is such a dominant topic and, if not properly understood and practiced, will overwhelm every other topic. So, it may be boring, but it is well worth it to understand the topic as best as you can.

My native country, the former United States of America, now a province of the USP, had a long history of elevating its government above its proper sphere. It was done by both those with Christian beliefs and those who held other beliefs. The Christians were largely just as guilty of misunderstanding this topic as others. Scholars debate why this was the case. Maybe I can offer some answers.

There were two main problems with how Americans had understood government. First, they understood government as a social contract to enforce a certain set of individual rights instead of a God-given call to promote and enforce biblically defined justice for all its peoples. Second, they practiced a functional state-religion that stifled true freedom of conscience and appropriate pluralism.[77]

Political science in the 18th Century was concerned with abandoning the old idea of the divine right of kings and replacing it with a rehashed version of the Greek idea of a social contract among rational citizens. John Locke is perhaps the man most responsible for formulating the ideas that are behind the American system. Setting up a system where the government's highest goals are the promotion and protection of individual rights naturally led to a battle over individual rights that led to the polarization and political disasters of the early 21st Century. It leads to many problems: If truths are self-evident, who is to say which are the most important? If I feel that my rights are being violated by your pursuit of your rights, why should we continue our social contract? If my rights as an individual are my highest priority, why should I care about other communities? In the end, politics became a matter of obtaining and holding power over those who would take away my individual rights and self-expression.

This first major problem: an ill-conceived political theory combined with the second major problem: lack of true religious pluralism. The United States was founded by people who had

---

[77] The idea of appropriate pluralism is based on the fact that Jesus sanctioned Caesar's role in government. The early Caesars were not Christian. Yet, they had a legitimate role in government. In this time between the first and second appearance of Christ, we must govern in a world of mixed world views, understanding non-Christians can have an important and God-sanctioned role in cooperative government.

not known a true pluralism of belief among its citizens but had existed as subjects of a monarch and responsible to a local theocracy of sorts.[78] They were not able to transition to the ideal they espoused. They inhibited true pluralism of belief, at least in the public realm. The history of religion in America is a history of one relatively monolithic state-approved religion after another.

At first, the heavily favored religion was a loose theism that is called Deism. It appears in many of the founding documents. It believed in a supreme being who largely left the management of his universe to the power of reason. So, when you read the Declaration of Independence, it mentions him as endowing rights that are self-evident, not rights that are given in the Bible or some other place but given via the power of reason – self-evident reasoning.

This Deism allowed public government-sponsored prayer, it required some Bible teaching and prayer in schools, it meant that successful politicians should be churchgoers. But it didn't want anything beyond that, it did not promote the authority of Jesus and his word, and it definitely didn't allow other religions that same sway that it had.[79]

---

[78] Stephen V. Monsma, J. Christopher Soper, The Challenge of Pluralism: Church and State in Five Democracies, Rowman & Littlefield, 1997

[79] Consider Stephen V. Monsma, J. Christopher Soper, The Challenge of Pluralism: Church and State in Five Democracies, Rowman & Littlefield, 1997

As the cultural elites became less Deistic and more functionally atheistic, the religion of Deism was replaced by an entirely secular state religion. And this religion held even greater sway than Deism ever did. The public arena of life was only friendly to a secular view.

The myth of secular-as-neutral took hold and effectively banished all true, free, and public exercise of religion to the personal and private parts of life.[80] You could worship in your church on Sunday and pray in private, but don't dare connect your political, educational, or professional pursuits with your religion. That was seen as abuse.

Mainstream science was the authority, government-run schools were the only schools that received tax dollars, educational curricula representing a secularist worldview was what had to be taught in these schools, most professions developed ethics that were devoid of any religious view other than the secular and humanist perspective.

Many, if not most Christians lived under these influences without ever realizing that they had been marginalized and silenced alongside any other faith or worldview that didn't endorse the secular view. And the government used all the power it could get to effectively squash any other approach to life.

---

[80] See Nancy Pearcey on this Pearcey, N. (2005). Total Truth. Crossway.

Wednesday, August 31st

I want to continue to talk about government, but I realize that I should try to concisely define secularism. I hope this will help clarify its effects and the proper response for followers of Jesus.[81]

Secularism is the perspective that humankind has an adequate ability and knowledge of truth to understand what it is to be human and how we should live. It stands on the assumption of the ability to figure out truth and goodness and noble goals through our own means. It rejects the need to appeal to a higher power or some source outside of what can be discovered through logic, common sense, reasonable philosophy, commonly held ethics, and science. It is the religion of the autonomy and adequacy of humans. Human reason and ability are sufficient for the order and flourishing of humankind in this view.

The problem with secularism isn't that it relies on reason and other human capabilities. The problem is that it exclusively relies on these and effectively and often completely rejects other means of acquiring truth and discovering pathways to flourishing. It also has historically demonstrated great animosity to fully-orbed Christianity and biblically-defined faith. It almost seems to have an ax to grind against the God of the Bible.

Back in the 20th century, it effectively won the place as the religion of state for the United States and many other

---

[81] See Smith, J. A. (2014). How (Not) to Be Secular. Wm. B. Eerdmans Publishing.

countries. Many Christians and people of other faiths conceded to its dominance and essentially compromised with it in the public square, in education, in the workplace, and even in their neighborhoods and among their friendships. To many observers, Christians appeared hardly different than their fully-secularized fellow citizens.

Thursday, September 1st

With all that I said yesterday, let's get back on track with talking about the government. As I said, many of the Christians back in the 20th and early 21st century didn't realize that they were walking into a big trap not only in their understanding of secularism but also in their understanding of government. Because of the historical tendency to look to the government to solve all the problems of society along with the United States' commitment to secularism as the state religion, just about any effort of the government, no matter how helpful, was ultimately undermining Christianity and Jesus' teaching on the place of government.

It wasn't so much the pervasive influence of the government but its displacing of other legitimate spheres. It is fitting for Caesar to have jurisdiction over collecting taxes, and establishing justice, and protecting people from injustice. All these are supported by scripture. But when Caesar tells people how to educate their children, what decisions parents are allowed, what level of income is legitimate, what professions are most favored, what religious views are allowed in public, etc., he has overstepped his bounds and taken territory God has not given him.

That other territory is the proper jurisdiction of the private sector, be it the family, schools, industry and agriculture, capital and labor, the arts, the sciences, education, or religion. These are all parallel spheres that must properly respect each other. The state has a reasonable role in these spheres to ensure basic justice, but not a role of ruling over any other sphere. The state can seek to empower these spheres and broker their cooperation, but not displace them. And each sphere must accommodate the legitimate, God-given role of the other spheres.

This approach was clarified and endorsed by the Council on Church & State, as I mentioned earlier.[82] Their extensive recommendations were instrumental in the reorganization of many governments after the collapse of Western Democracy as we had known it. The historical commitment to overly dominant governments alongside the confusion and polarization caused by the bankruptcy of secularism was like two explosive chemicals mixed together and shaken up. After the explosion, almost nothing was left.

When we tried to pick up the pieces, the extremely winsome and comprehensive recommendations of the Council were there to help form new governments and even societies based on these Christian principles of governance that allowed for a

---

[82] See Some Mouw, Richard J., 1998, Reflections on Sphere Sovereignty, The Princeton Seminary Bulletin, Vol 19, Issue 2, p 160-182. See: https://ia801206.us.archive.org/35/items/princetonsemi-nar1921prin/princetonseminar1921prin.pdf

thriving principled pluralism that blessed us for so many years.[83]

Friday, September 2nd

You may be wondering what this government model looked like. At the core of the political theory under this new arrangement was the biblical truth on the role of the state. One of the most influential verses is Romans 13:1-5.[84] This section of scripture makes it clear that the governing authorities are given the right to bring punishment to wrongdoers that good might be upheld. They are tasked with upholding good and punishing evil, of promoting God's system of justice. They are not chiefly charged with upholding individual rights. They are not to serve themselves. They are not to exercise authority outside of the realm that God has assigned. They do not serve a mere social contract. They have an obligation to God himself and the good of the whole society. These truths both appropriately expand

---

[83] Consider current similar political approaches held by the American Solidarity Party and some Christian Democratic parties.

[84] 1 Let every person be subject to the governing authorities. For there is no authority except from God, and those that exist have been instituted by God. 2 Therefore whoever resists the authorities resists what God has appointed, and those who resist will incur judgment. 3 For rulers are not a terror to good conduct, but too bad. Would you have no fear of the one who is in authority? Then do what is good, and you will receive his approval, 4 for he is God's servant for your good. But if you do wrong, be afraid, for he does not bear the sword in vain. For he is the servant of God, an avenger who carries out God's wrath on the wrongdoer. 5 Therefore one must be in subjection, not only to avoid God's wrath but also for the sake of conscience. (Romans 13:1–5, ESV)

and properly limit the role of government. And because the government functions this way in parallel with other God-ordained social institutions, the historical battles on the size and scope of the government were effectively settled.

So, the governments still collect revenue mostly through taxes on the appropriate services, commerce and goods, sorry to disappoint. But they didn't need as much money, at least in the NAU (North American Union.) Social welfare programs were greatly transformed and enhanced by the government restructuring public assistance for the poor, disabled, unemployed, and the elderly. They did supply a portion of money and effort in these areas, but this was largely managed alongside the funds coming from other spheres not under the control of the government. There was large-scale and successful cooperation with other sectors of society such as churches, synagogues, mosques, labor unions, businesses, and charitable organizations of various kinds. Additionally, the governments of the provinces and municipalities did the same.

Through private contributions, religious and civic, local and provincial programs and a better-defined federal involvement, all under the influence of a freely offered and freely imbibed Christian social ethic, the various basic needs were well met. This combined system led to all segments experiencing a much higher level of care and quality of life.

This was the same in health insurance, something previously overwhelming for the government and society as a whole. This approach allowed cost sharing and cost reduction for health care costs. It also brought greater responsibility to litigation and lawyers' actions by bringing influence and accountability from the other spheres. Of course, the big leaps forward in science also greatly reduced the incidence of many sicknesses that previously were costly and deadly.

The tenor of politics greatly shifted. We no longer were expecting the government to solve all our problems. We no longer were fighting each other over individual rights. The government was seen as an equal partner with other spheres in promoting a just and prosperous society. They were more fully supported as a partner alongside other spheres of society.

There was a massive improvement in the cost and quality of education. Many new colleges and universities were started, all competing to be places of educational excellence, preparing the very best citizens to serve the common good. Education was no longer the purview of the government, but government tax money was used to supplement personal funds for the underprivileged. This way, every student could pick from an array of options and receive the very best education available to them.

All schools became essentially private. All schools could teach what they wanted but had to cover basics like math, science, literature, and language, ethics, and metaphysics if they wanted to receive government assistance. But the particular worldviews behind these different subjects could be from any religion or philosophy as long as it didn't endorse violation of the central ethics of the government, which were determined as the core ethics for the entire population.

These core ethics for the North American Union were understood as given by God, not merely determined by popular consent. Law as popular consent was a great failure in Western history.[85] The key God-given laws were distilled as follows: 1. Honor God Above All 2. Honor Marriage and Family 3. Honor and Protect All Human Life 4. Promote Truth 5. Support Your Neighbor and His Communities 6. Respect Personal Dignity & Conscience 7. Respect Personal Property. These helped greatly to guide our union and create a context for mutual thriving and respect.[86]

The government largely divested of regulating industry apart from issues related to public justice and safety as defined by the core ethics. Industry-specific guilds and unions were created to oversee their respective areas. These guilds were self-regulating in many ways. The government sought to facilitate their cooperation, and many mutually beneficial agreements were enacted between the various guilds and unions. Of course, the consumers formed one of the most powerful unions, and their influence was powerful in helping industries and laborers remember who they were seeking to benefit.

The benefit to the arts and sciences was tremendous. With the tax burden greatly reduced and a Christian ethic holding much sway, people and various institutions were more than eager to contribute to all sorts of arts programs and worthy scientific pursuits. Many people who previously had to keep their pursuit of music or fine art as a hobby now could find full employment in using their gifts. The result was a wonderful

---

[85] See Nancy Pearcey on this Pearcey, N. (2005). Total Truth. Chapter 8: Darwins of the Mind, Crossway

[86] Compare with Exodus 20:1-17, Matthew 22:35-40.

golden age of art and music surpassing anything the renaissance ever saw.

I have already shared the benefits in science. So many new research agencies were formed and funded. There was tremendous progress in medicine, biotech, electronics, space travel, astrophysics, chemistry, manufacturing technology, environmental sciences, food production, and many other areas. This all came from allowing these spheres to act relatively independently and unencumbered by government involvement while being held properly accountable by the other spheres.

Of course, the churches and religious groups thrived under this new system. But I will cover more of that tomorrow.

Saturday, September 3rd

When the governments reformed, there was a commitment to pursue a "principled pluralism." It was principled because there were basic ethics and commitments to the government that were understood as given by God himself and from a core, commonly-held Christian perspective. It was pluralism because it was committed to freedom of conscience and true and full participation by people from diverse backgrounds.

Previously, the United States of America practiced a sort of separation of church and state that was not pluralism but the exclusion from state functions of all religious worldviews other than secularism. Freedom of religion was really freedom from religion in all spheres but private and personal spheres. It was not expected that someone could participate in public life while fully sharing and living from their faith. They had to check those things and learn to get along with the state religion. This was not freedom of religion.

With the new Union of North America, various worldviews were accepted, respected, and expected to contribute their voice in the discussion of various issues in the various spheres, including government. Christians of various particular convictions, Jewish people, Muslims, Buddhists, Atheists, and Animists were all allowed to practice their faith without shame and create their own educational institutions, art, science, and social foundations.

The polarization of politics was greatly reduced through these practices. Because the sphere of religion was now greatly respected and supported without government interference, there were fewer issues in politics to divide over. People didn't expect the government to solve the social, religious, and ethical issues of the world. They had to work with the influence of religious groups and stay out of areas that were no longer their purview. The subsequently reduced tax burden along with this change of mindset greatly increased charitable giving, and all religious groups did better under these principles.

The Christian church did very well. Contributions increased at least five-fold topping off at $10 trillion per year. A renewed effort to create healthy, thriving churches among all peoples and in all the villages of the world took off. This effort alone, humanly speaking, radically changed the world in our lifetime.

Sunday, September 4th

Although the government was not as influential after the Cataclysm and reconstruction, it still had an important place in society. As Christians, we are commanded to pray for governing authorities, honor them, and submit to their authority. Let me share for this Sunday entry a liturgy for those who work in government. Please take time to pray through this for those who serve in your government and for your nation.

A Liturgy for Our Government & Its Leaders[87]

O Lord, the Supreme Governor, bless the leaders of our land, that we may be a people at peace among ourselves and a blessing to other nations of the earth.

All: Lord, keep this nation under your care

To the Prime Minister and members of the Cabinet, to Governors of States, Mayors of Cities, and to all in administrative authority, grant wisdom and grace in the exercise of their duties.

All: Give grace to your servants, O Lord.

To Senators and Representatives, and those who make our laws in States, Cities, and Towns, give them respect for other authorities, grant them courage, wisdom, and foresight to so serve in their role as to provide for the peace and protection of

---

[87] Adapted from the Book of Common Prayer, Prayers and Thanksgiving, Item 22, Prayer for Sound Government. See
https://www.bcponline.org/Misc/Prayers.html

our people, and to fulfill our obligations in the community of nations.

All: *Give grace to your servants, O Lord.*

To the Judges and officers of our Courts give understanding and integrity, that human rights may be safeguarded and you're your truth and justice upheld.

All: *Give grace to your servants, O Lord.*

And finally, teach us, your people to trust in you first and foremost. Grant all of us strength to accept our responsibilities to our fellow citizens, that they may elect trustworthy leaders and make wise decisions for the well-being of our society; that we may serve you faithfully in our generation and honor your holy Name.

All: *For yours is the kingdom, O Lord, and you are exalted as head above all. Amen.*

Chapter 5: The Pain and Pleasure of Living

Monday, September 5th

Woke up this morning feeling really anxious and fearful. I don't know why. I had terrible feelings of dread and failure. Am I getting this all wrong? Am I just being proud and inflexible? Am I bringing all this pain into everybody's lives because I am just stubborn?

And then my mind goes in another direction. What if they do this to Abby? What if the grandkids suffer, too? What if they torture my sweet wife and sweet little grandchildren? What if I am wrong and God himself is angry with me? Why am I throwing away so much good? Why can't I just learn to get along with others?

And then wave upon wave of fear, anxiety, terror, and cold sweats sweep over me, and I feel like I am going to vomit and lose my mind at the same time. And I feel trapped all by myself with my thoughts, all alone here in my cell with just me and my feeble brain, aging body, and my lonely soul.

I am not new to these feelings, but they are more intense than ever. It feels that if they continue, I will lose my sanity and be an utter failure, a pathetic lunatic who deserved to be broken in mind and body for his sociopathic stubbornness.

Where is God in all this? Where are his promises? Where is the Good Shepherd who is supposed to be with me through the valley of the Shadow of Death? How can a good God allow such terrible feelings? How can a good God allow such terrible circumstances? Why has he unleashed such pain and suffering upon his creation? How can he possibly be good and in control if there is such brokenness and evil in his creation?

Oh, God, please help me. Oh, God, please answer. Oh God, please rescue me from these feelings. Oh God, please keep me and guard me against all evil. Oh, God, help me. Please, help me.

Tuesday, September 6th

Went to bed last night with this verse on my mind. *"I have told you all this so that you may have peace in me. Here on earth you will have many trials and sorrows. But take heart, because I have overcome the world."*[88] I recited it over and over and prayed through it again and again with many tears and groans and specific requests for loved ones and even my enemies. I was able to sleep most of the night and woke up feeling much better. I can still feel the anxiety attacks getting ready to erupt but have been able to overcome them and experience peace.

What an amazing verse. Jesus had been speaking words to his disciples about the Father and the Spirit and their relationship with the disciples along with Jesus. He was about to go through his crucifixion and then, after his resurrection, his physical departure and ascension. He wanted them to have peace amidst all the upheaval they would be going through.

Jesus, God himself, in the flesh, tells them that in this world, they will have many trials and sorrows. Jesus knew this as God

---

[88] John 16:33

and as the one who would go through the greatest trial and sorrow – his crucifixion on the cross. It would drive him to pray so intensely that night that he would actually sweat and bleed. He would go to the cross and cry out in his sorrow, "My God, my God, why have you forsaken me?" He who knew no sin would become sin for us on the cross. He would bear the holy justice of God and be pierced for our transgressions, crushed for our iniquities, chastised for our peace, wounded for our healing. It was the will of the Lord to crush him. God has put him to grief. Out of the anguish of his soul, he shall see and be satisfied with what he has done.[89]

Jesus is no stranger to suffering and sorrow. This amazing verse from John 16 is so helpful. In it, we know that God has designed that suffering and sorrow shall happen in his universe. He has even designed that evil shall be allowed and have its effects. Yet, he doesn't do so to stand aloof but to enter the deepest part of the fray and experience the consequences in the most dramatic way. And as he does so, he overcomes this evil, this brokenness, this suffering, this sorrow. He turns all of it into redemption and victory in a totally unexpected way. He wins by losing. And he wins completely.

This is what helped me to take heart. This is what helped me to not despise my weakness, my sufferings, my sorrow. I belong to him, and in him, these things are made to show that I can overcome the world, too, even when it throws its worst at me. God has designed it so. God has designed my redemption to

---

[89] Isaiah 53:1-11

work in and through my sufferings as I am held by Jesus, the overcomer.[90]

Wednesday, September 7th

Still able to get some good sleep at night. I am very grateful. I was thinking about the flip side of suffering – enjoyment and pleasure. If we are going to ask what the purpose of suffering is, we should also ask what the purpose of pleasure is. I think more people are sidetracked by the improper handling of pleasure vs. suffering.

Pleasure is the sense we get when we are pleased. Pleasure can be a physical sensation, an emotional experience, a spiritual high, intellectual satisfaction, and more. Pleasure is any sort of experience that would please our body or soul.

Pleasure is not synonymous with goodness. We don't experience pleasure only when good things are happening to us or others. And pleasure isn't necessarily good in and of itself. It can be a pleasing experience that is terribly destructive, such as overdosing on heroin. If we merely seek to maximize our pleasure, we will likely do much evil, not good.

It is this disconnect between the pleasurable and the good that can get us into a lot of trouble. Yet, we need to be careful not to disconnect the good and the pleasurable. As a matter of

---

[90] "My sheep listen to my voice; I know them, and they follow me. I give them eternal life, and they will never perish. No one can snatch them away from me," (John 10:27–28)

fact, the pathway to ultimate good is through realigning what we truly believe and experience as most pleasing.

There are two Bible passages that shed much light on this topic. First, Genesis 3. It says:

> [1] *Now the serpent was more crafty than any other beast of the field that the LORD God had made. He said to the woman, "Did God actually say, 'You shall not eat of any tree in the garden'?"* [2] *And the woman said to the serpent, "We may eat of the fruit of the trees in the garden,* [3] *but God said, 'You shall not eat of the fruit of the tree that is in the midst of the garden, neither shall you touch it, lest you die.'* [4] *But the serpent said to the woman, "You will not surely die.* [5] *For God knows that when you eat of it your eyes will be opened, and you will be like God, knowing good and evil."* [6] *So when the woman saw that the tree was good for food, and that it was a delight to the eyes, and that the tree was to be desired to make one wise, she took of its fruit and ate, and she also gave some to her husband who was with her, and he ate.*

Genesis 3:1–6 (ESV)

This is the famous temptation of Adam and Eve by the Devil. I can't get into everything that is here, but I want to focus on how Eve evaluated what to do. The serpent asserted that God's warning about the fruit was false, and his prohibition was hiding an ulterior motive. Eve responded in three ways. She saw that the fruit was good. She saw that it was pleasing. And she believed the serpent's claims were true. So, seeing it as true, good, and pleasing, she ate.

73

Now, take a look at Romans 12:1-2.

> *And so, dear brothers and sisters, I plead with you to give your bodies to God because of all he has done for you. Let them be a living and holy sacrifice – the kind he will find acceptable. This is truly the way to worship him. Don't copy the behavior and customs of this world, but let God transform you into a new person by changing the way you think. Then you will learn to know God's will for you, which is good and pleasing and perfect.*

> Romans 12:1–2

This verse is kind of the mirror image for the Genesis 3 passage. Genesis 3 is falling into evil and death, and Romans 12 is being lifted out of evil into true life. Here Paul is telling the Romans that they are to present themselves as living sacrifices to God because of all he has done for us in Christ. And as part of that lifestyle of worship and service to God, we are to be transformed by a renewal of our perspective that as we learn the truth and apply it, we might discern that the will of God is good, pleasing, and perfect. So, we learn that God's will is good, pleasing, and complete (comprehensively right in every way, including robustly true.)

So, the point in using both these passages is to show that you will choose what you think maximizes the combination of true, good, and pleasing. So, the pathway to ultimate truth and goodness involves ultimate pleasure. We will always seek to maximize this combination in everything we do. The key is to pick that which most maximizes these over the long haul.

Too often, we seek to maximize one of these qualities over another. Or we seek to maximize our temporary experience of these versus our long-term experience of them. This behavior can lead to great evil, Adam and Eve being a prime example. Every human being's failure and sin continues to illustrate the same principle. And every follower of Christ's growth in Christlikeness also illustrates this principle.[91]

Pleasure is meant to function as part of our choices and our pursuits but in its proper place alongside truth and goodness. And our pleasure must not simply be a physical pleasure or an emotional pleasure or a spiritual pleasure. It should be a fully-orbed and maximized pleasure involving our whole being, body, and soul, in relationship with the Trinity and with those made in his image, all as a part of his overall creation. All these factors must be considered when pursuing true and maximum pleasure.

Thursday, September 8th

Sorry if yesterday was too abstract. I figured I would give some practical illustrations from the Bible and from life today.

Jesus says in John 8:29, "*I always do the things that are pleasing to him.*" And it says in John 4:31-34, "*Meanwhile, the disciples were urging Jesus, 'Rabbi, eat something.' But Jesus replied, 'I have a kind of food you know nothing about.' 'Did someone bring him food while we were gone?' the disciples asked each other. Then Jesus explained: 'My*

---

[91] Consider Thomas Chalmers, The Expulsive Power of a New Affection, Crossway, 2020

nourishment comes from doing the will of God, who sent me, and from finishing his work.' "[92]

These verses show that Jesus was oriented towards pleasing the Father and doing his will in such a powerful way that he craved it more than physical food for a hungry body. We all know how pleasing good food is when you are really hungry. But for Jesus, the good food of his father's good, pleasing, and perfect will was more desirable than regular food.

I think we experience the same sort of thing in ordinary life. I really like chocolate, and anything made of chocolate. I love the sort of chocolate brownies that are almost like fudge, chewy, and filled with chocolate and chocolate chips. I love when they come out of the oven, and the smell is so good and strong you could serve it on a plate, too. It is hard to resist these sorts of brownies. But, if I know that they are being made for sharing with our neighbors who just went through the tragic loss of a grandparent and have had a season of sickness and un-employment, I can resist eating them and even enjoy my abstinence. And so, my enjoyment of brownies is channeled to my enjoyment of our friends being blessed by those brownies and enjoying them not only for the brownies' innate goodness but because they represent our love and care for them. The pleasure in blessing our neighbors exceeds the pleasure of eating the brownies. So, I am able to choose the better.

Similarly, in every challenging ethical decision in life, where God tells me to do something I might not immediately prefer

---

[92] John 4:31–34

or even might bring suffering or privation of pleasure, I can trust that in the long haul, that decision will maximize true and good pleasure.

Take sex as an example. Our bodies are made to feel pleasure with sexual activity. There are nerve endings, hormones, biochemistry, and neurological phenomena of all sorts tied into the experience of sex. It is perhaps the most pleasurable experience a human can have. There are all sorts of possible ways that we can maximize the experience of sexual pleasure.

Yet, sexual experience involves a human being, made in the image of God, body, and soul. There is much more to a human being than simply the sexual response. And the experience of sexual pleasure is connected to a human in all of the depth and breadth of their humanity. (Their humanity is this profound because it is an image of God himself.) And if we only consider sexual pleasure, we are missing out on all the other dimensions of pleasure and reality for us as humans.

So, God teaches us that sex is meant to function in a context. There are both encouragements and prohibitions in biblical sexual ethics. There is one whole book of the Bible dedicated to the enjoyment of sex within marriage. Yet, there are prohibitions on having sex outside of marriage. This is given because there are many other aspects of our humanity that must be considered alongside our sexual pleasure. And sexual pleasure is designed to function in the context of a lifelong covenant between a man and a woman. And the pursuit of sexual pleasure outside of the context given in scripture will do more harm than good, to the point of destroying the image of God we all bear.

Sex is a pleasure that builds and celebrates true and complete human union. This union only happens within the covenant of marriage. Yet marriage is not the end but a means to point to the deeper union of Christ with his people.[93] Giving oneself to the ultimate union of Christ and his church is part of how all believers, married or single people can direct their sexual energy – towards contributing in a feminine or masculine way, respectively, towards a deeper holy communion of brothers and sisters in the Church.

So, when we consider the greater context of our choices: what is good, pleasing, and true, we will be able to better maximize the positive impact of our actions and avoid things that would bring harm and offense to our relationship with God and with others.

Friday, September 9th

I thought that today I would journal about addictions. Addictions are the abuse of pleasure. Addictions have always been a problem for people. They peaked as a problem in the first half of the 21st century. Addictions to opiates, alcohol, and sex were so common. It was reported that at any given time, up to 20% of those over 12 years old struggled with alcohol or drug abuse.[94] As many as 16% of the population struggled with sex

---

[93] See Ephesians 5:22-33.

[94] See National Survey on Drug Use and Health, https://www.samhsa.gov/data/sites/default/files/cbhsq-reports/NSDUHNationalFindingsReport2018/NSDUHNationalFindingsReport2018.pdf

addiction.[95] The impact of addictions seemed worst among young people.[96] This was likely because they, most of all, felt the effects of our fractured, divided, cynical, and lonely society.

Addictions have two components that must both be considered in overcoming them. First, addictions are idolatry. They are a sickness of the soul. They are sin against God and others.[97] The dangerous substance or lifestyle serves as the source and goal of the addict's life. They find some sort of deep, life-giving satisfaction in the destructive substance or behavior, and they orient their life around maintaining their addictive lifestyle. Often this addictive lifestyle is very destructive to the addict's relationships with others and the normal social contexts of a stable life. They too often sacrifice friendships, family, marriage, employment, and community for the sake of pursuing their addiction. Treatment centers are full of people who once had very successful and admirable lives. The substance or behavior has become their god. They are worshippers of the wrong thing. The result is catastrophic.

---

[95] Laurent Karila et al, Sexual Addiction or Hypersexual Disorder: Different Terms for the Same Problem? A Review of the Literature, Current Pharmaceutical Design, 2014, 20, 000-000, see http://www.uclep.be/wp-content/uploads/pdf/Pub/Karila_CPD_2014.pdf

[96] Alcohol and Drug Misuse and Suicide and the Millennial Generation – a Devastating Impact, Trust for America's Health (TFAH), https://wellbeingtrust.org/wp-content/uploads/2019/06/TFAH-2019-YoundAdult-Pain-Brief-FnlRv.pdf

[97] Consider Welch, E. T. (2001). Addictions: A banquet in the grave: Finding hope in the power of the Gospel. Phillipsburg, New Jersey: P & R Pub.

Second, addictions are a sickness of the body. Addictions are physiological phenomena where the body is rewired according to the biochemical effects of the abuse of the substance or lifestyle. There is some experience of pleasure in the addiction that is at a bodily level. Brain imaging has shown that addicts' brains change in the sections related to judgment, decision making, learning, memory, and behavior control.[98,99] Additionally, various neurotransmitters are manipulated by addictions and may play a dominant role in addictive behavior.[100]

Accordingly, successful treatment must address both aspects and bring change and healing to body and soul. The body needs to be healed and rehabilitated, and the person's soul needs to be revitalized and learn to be truly satisfied in God and his kingdom. The addict must be totally rehabilitated from his or her former abuse of pleasure to a new experience of death to selfish pleasures and pursuit of appropriate pleasures aligned in worship to God. He or she must experience the "expulsive power of a superior affection" as Thomas Chalmers put it so long ago.[101] That is, the addict must find something that is truly

---

[98] Fowler, J. S., Volkow, N. D., Kassed, C. A., & Chang, L. (2007). Imaging the addicted human brain. Science & practice perspectives, 3(2), 4–16. https://doi.org/10.1151/spp07324

[99] https://www.psychiatry.org/patients-families/addiction/what-is-addiction

[100] Koob, G. F., & Simon, E. J. (2009). The Neurobiology of Addiction: Where We Have Been and Where We Are Going. Journal of drug issues, 39(1), 115–132. https://doi.org/10.1177/002204260903900110

[101] Thomas Chalmers, The Expulsive Power of a New Affection, Crossway, 2020

and thoroughly better to replace the addiction. This, of course will be found as the addict believes and embraces a Christ-centered lifestyle that encompasses body and soul. Both body and soul have to be addressed for the recovery from addiction.

Saturday, September 10th

Thankfully, the Council on Redemption & Sanctification invested heavily in addressing this rampant problem and provided some substantial, culture-changing help in this area. They recognized the soul-body connection at play in addictions and recommended principles of treatment, rehabilitation, and long-term lifestyle that we found miraculously redemptive in addressing this chronic sin and disease.

The outline of their encyclical calls for the addicted individual to process through 12 key steps in addressing addiction, similar to the 12 steps used by Alcoholics Anonymous but amended to provide a more robustly Christian plan of full recovery.

1. *We must admit that we have sinned and given ourselves over to idolatry and disease, which oppose God, destroy us and bring harm to those we love.*
2. *We confess that the Triune God is able and eager to help us overcome this sin and disease as we depend on him. We recognize that God provides both the Church and qualified medical programs as keys to the recovery of body and soul.*
3. *We have decided to turn away from this sin and disease and turn our lives over to God himself, to rescue us, redeem us and remake us as he pleases.*

4. *We receive the atoning sacrifice of Christ, which pays for all our sins and brings full redemption. We rest in his righteousness, mercy, and love as our only hope. We receive our new identity as beloved saints of God rescued from sin for a life of love, service and suffering for his name.*[102]

5. *We have joined a local church to find support and opportunities for service in the new life of freedom from addiction. We have enrolled in the treatment programs necessary for our full recovery in body and soul.*

6. *We have been honest and comprehensive in addressing all our sins and shortcomings before God, our loved ones, and our local church.*

7. *We pledge to work with God to change in every area of life and make restitution for any damage done to others as far as we are able.*

8. *We participate with a local organization such as the Order of the Redeemed Life (ORL) for mutual support, Christian growth, and active service under the auspices of our local churches.*[103]

---

[102] "My old self has been crucified with Christ. It is no longer I who live, but Christ lives in me. So I live in this earthly body by trusting in the Son of God, who loved me and gave himself for me." (Galatians 2:20)

[103] This Order was created as a Christian discipleship and service vehicle to further growth and missional community amidst the disorder and challenges of our modern, fragmented society. It helps provide the structure of Christian life and service once inherent in the lifestyles built around local village living or monastic community. It's implementation by the Council has been very successful both in treating addictions and serving the broader community with Christian love and gospel mission. Compare it to the structure and influence of AA in helping addicts abstain from their addictions through an analogous approach. The AA approach lacks the robust Christian viewpoint presented here.

9. *We regularly engage in prayer, Bible reading, confession, and encouragement through participation in the meetings during the regular offices prepared by our local ORL or other means, either in person or electronically.*[104]
10. *We regularly look to use our time, talents, and resources to help other people as we acknowledge that true life is found by dying to self and living in Jesus for others' benefit.*[105] *We serve on a weekly basis in our local church and other ministries such as a local ORL.*

---

[104]This would include at least 4 of the traditional offices: 1. Dawn, 2. Prime (before work – usually 7 am), 3. Midmorning (9 or 10 AM), 4. Noon , 5. Midafternoon (3 PM), 6. Vespers (sunset, approximately 6 p.m.), 7. Compline (end of the day before retiring, approximately 9 p.m.), 8. Vigil (middle of the night – usually 2 a.m.) and 9. Matins (a later portion of Vigil, from 3 a.m. to dawn). The most commonly attended are Prime, Noon, Vespers and Compline. Consider the scriptural warrant for regular hours of prayer and devotion: Daniel 6:10, Luke 1:10, Acts 3:1, 10:3,30, 1 Thess 5:17, Col 3:16-17. Compare the models presented by a) Justin Whitmel Earley, "The Common Rule," IVP, Downers Grove, Illinois, 2019, or b) Keller, Timothy J., Prayer: Experiencing Awe and Intimacy with God, Penguin Books, 2014, p. 240ff and c) "Morning Quiet Time" practiced by the majority of evangelicals.

[105] "Then he said to the crowd, "If any of you wants to be my follower, you must give up your own way, take up your cross daily, and follow me. If you try to hang on to your life, you will lose it. But if you give up your life for my sake, you will save it. And what do you benefit if you gain the whole world but are yourself lost or destroyed?" (Luke 9:23–25)

"I tell you the truth, unless a kernel of wheat is planted in the soil and dies, it remains alone. But its death will produce many new kernels – a plentiful harvest of new lives. Those who love their life in this world will lose it. Those who care nothing for their life in this world will keep it for eternity. Anyone who wants to serve me must follow me, because my servants must

11. *We recognize that God's word speaks authoritatively over our lives in identifying our problems, offering real solutions, and providing for a new life, identity, purpose, and destiny for all who believe.*

12. *We recognize that our choices and actions will shape the world we live in now and determine the eternal destiny of our lives, so we soberly pledge to walk out these steps together and in fear of God and the hope of the gospel and the world to come.*

Sunday, September 11th

I include a selection from a liturgy for my Sunday post. I have found this liturgy to be very helpful when struggling with temptations to do something impulsive. There were days when I prayed through this ten times or more throughout the day.

A Liturgy for One Battling a Destructive Desire[106]

Jesus, here I am again,
desiring a thing
that were I to indulge in it
would war against my own heart,
and the hearts of those I love.

---

be where I am. And the Father will honor anyone who serves me." (John 12:24–26)

"My old self has been crucified with Christ. It is no longer I who live, but Christ lives in me. So, I live in this earthly body by trusting in the Son of God, who loved me and gave himself for me." (Galatians 2:20)

[106] A Liturgy for One Battling a Destructive Desire, Douglas McKelvey, Every Moment Holy, Rabbit Room Press (2017)

O Christ, rather let my life be thine!

Take my desires. Let them be subsumed
in still greater desire for you,
until there remains no room
for these lesser cravings.

In this moment I might choose
to indulge a fleeting hunger,
or I might choose
to love you more.

Faced with this temptation,
I would rather choose you, Jesus –

But I am weak. So be my strength·

I am shadowed. Be my light.

I am selfish. Unmake me now,
and refashion my desires
according to the better designs of your love.

Given the choice of shame or glory,
let me choose glory.

Given the choice of this moment or eternity,
let me choose in this moment what is eternal.

Given the choice of this easy pleasure,
or the harder road of the cross,
give me grace to choose to follow you,
knowing that there is nowhere apart from your

presence where I might find the peace I long for,
no lasting satisfaction apart from your
reclamation of my heart.

Let me build, then, my King,
a beautiful thing by long obedience,
by the steady progression of small choices
that laid end to end will become like the stones
of a pleasing path stretching to eternity and
unto your welcoming arms and unto the sound
of your voice pronouncing the judgment:

Well done

Chapter 6: Not Meant to Be Alone

Monday, September 12th

I had a wonderful time yesterday with Abby. The prison system allows a private visit with your spouse after a month of good behavior. They provide a hotel-like suite with a little courtyard that even has a garden. It is a rare privilege, and we took full advantage of the time. We were able to order in a catered meal from a local restaurant. I was given some real clothes to wear instead of the usual prison orange jumpsuit I wear every other day.

Abby wore a gorgeous purple outfit, with a matching headband that made her blue eyes glow like the deep indigo of the Caribbean on a sunny day. She was so beautiful. It was like our second honeymoon. We treasured every moment. We talked, we ate our meal. We listened to our favorite music, we sang harmony together. We prayed together. We laughed at so many things, and we cried and even sobbed together. We recited our favorite poetry and hymns. We held hands. And we enjoyed wonderful sexual intimacy. All of that was packed into about four hours. But it seemed like a whole weekend.

I can't imagine loving anybody more than Abby. Not that it has always been easy. We have needed to work on so many things. We both have needed to learn to die to our own preferences, to apologize more than demand, to give more than take, to delight in the other more than ourselves, to forgive much, to pray much, to get lots of help, and keep on working on our marriage. But the fruit of seeking the kingdom of God this way has created a friendship, an intimacy, a partnership, and a mutual joy that is more than worth all the pain of killing selfishness, granting forgiveness, and just simple hard work.

The thought of losing her and saying goodbye is like a horrible lead weight on my soul. I feel ill just thinking about it. I am so deeply grieved at the prospect of ending our very special union of the past 40 years. We have been together so long that it will be like ripping both of us in half. I can't really deal with thinking about it too much. It's overwhelming.

O God, help us. O God, who created us male and female, who called us as husband and wife to cleave to each other and become one flesh, please help us as they tear us apart. O God, we have been together since we were so young. How can we be apart now? O God, we know you are bigger and greater than this tragedy. We know that you designed marriage as a great blessing but only a mere reflection of our eternal union with you in paradise. Please grant us real hope and peace we can feel. We need these from you in order to deal with this. We can only trust you to make good on your word. We must believe that you have something better ahead. O, grant us strength. O grant us help. This is tearing us into pieces.

Tuesday, September 13th

It was so wonderful to have those four hours with Abby on Sunday. I struggled yesterday thinking more about losing her. But gratefulness for over 40 years of marriage and countless hours together over that time has helped me feel better. And the truth that earthly marriage is at the very best a dim reflection of the wonderful union we have with God for eternity has given me hope for the future. Although we won't be husband and wife as we have known it on the earth, we will be one with the Lord and, through that, one with each other in God. The erotic and coital aspect of our union will be absent,[107] but there will be a deep and holy spiritual union in God.[108] Remembering all we have experienced together and knowing all we will experience together has been really helpful.

Marriage is really an amazing thing. It fell into disrepute in the early 21st century, and the result was catastrophic. It wasn't just marriage that disintegrated; it was the very core of our understanding of what it is to be human. When gender and sexual preference were considered fluid, it led to our human identity being fluid. But God clearly reveals who we are in the very beginning of the Bible. He says in Genesis 1:

> *"Then God said, "Let us make human beings in our image, to be like us. They will reign over the fish in the sea, the birds in the sky, the livestock, all the wild animals on the earth, and the small animals that scurry along the ground." So, God created*

---

[107] "For when the dead rise, they will neither marry nor be given in marriage. In this respect they will be like the angels in heaven." (Matthew 22:30)

[108] "I am praying not only for these disciples but also for all who will ever believe in me through their message. 21 I pray that they will all be one, just as you and I are one – as you are in me, Father, and I am in you. And may they be in us so that the world will believe you sent me." (John 17:20–21)

human beings in his own image. In the image of God he created them; male and female he created them."[109]

This verse outlines the core of what it is to be human. I covered it back in August. But it is really important to understand that God does not make mankind a singularity. He makes them a binary, male or female. This correlates with the "us" of verse 25. To be made in the image of God is to be made like the "us." God is not a single person but three persons profoundly united in one being. It is hard for us to understand. But this is why he has made us male and female – to express the diversity and unity that is part of the Godhead. Men and women are purposely different from one another yet called to unity.

How are they different? That is a key question. It seemed pretty obvious to Adam and Eve, and it has seemed pretty obvious to thousands of generations before us. But, somehow, we had trouble recently.[110] The effect of radical feminism and the strong agenda of the LGBTQ+ radicals did much to bring confusion to something that is normally very clear. This recent decline seems to track what Paul talks about in Romans 1.

> *"And instead of worshiping the glorious, ever-living God, they worshiped idols made to look like mere people and birds and animals and reptiles. So, God abandoned them to do whatever shameful things their hearts desired. As a result, they did vile and degrading things with each other's bodies. They traded the*

---

[109] Genesis 1:16

[110] See the discussion in "Chapter 12: How Women Started the Culture War" by Nancy Pearcey, Total Truth, (p. 325). Crossway. Kindle Edition.

truth about God for a lie. So, they worshiped and served the things God created instead of the Creator himself, who is worthy of eternal praise! Amen. That is why God abandoned them to their shameful desires. Even the women turned against the natural way to have sex and instead indulged in sex with each other. And the men, instead of having normal sexual relations with women, burned with lust for each other. Men did shameful things with other men, and as a result of this sin, they suffered within themselves the penalty they deserved. Since they thought it foolish to acknowledge God, he abandoned them to their foolish thinking and let them do things that should never be done.[III]"

Of course, all rebellion against God is wrong, whether it is sexual deviancy or gossip. But some sins are more destructive than others. And it certainly seems from scripture and experience that sin against one's body in terms of sexual immorality is destructive to society and the individual. They twist something that is meant to be glorious and profound and holy. More about that tomorrow. My mind is tired today.

Wednesday, September 14

All right, after a pretty good night's rest, I'm ready to journal some more on human sexuality today. I don't have time here to get into everything the Bible and the Council on Humankind stated on human sexuality. But I think I can sum up based on what we see in Genesis. Eve is called to be Adam's helper. Adam is called to lead in their mission. Together they are to rule over all of creation, be fruitful, and multiply. There is a similarity in

---

[III] Romans 1:23–28

their mission but a difference in orientation. Adam is oriented to lead in response to God's call. Eve is oriented towards helping Adam in response to his leadership. While it is important not to overstate these differences to the point where the man dominates, and the woman is a robotic slave, it is also important to clearly see that there is a difference in orientation toward their mandate to rule and image God. The man is to be an initiator, taking responsibility, planning, and accomplishing tasks that are part of imaging God. The woman is a responder to the man's initiative bringing essential assistance in nurturing, supporting, and complementing the man in his role.[112]

This paradigm certainly fits with the biological differences between men and women. Men's bodies are made for strength. Their genitalia are made to initiate life but not sustain it. Their minds are made for focusing on narrow tasks. Their masculine energy will propel them to work hard to accomplish tasks. Women's bodies are strong but made for producing and nurturing children. Their genitalia are made for receiving a man's initiative of life and sustaining it. Their minds are capable of significant multitasking, especially tasks that build relationships and community. It seems consistent to see a continuity from the biology of the sexes into the general roles of the sexes.

This doesn't mean that every job is either masculine or feminine. There are probably very few jobs that the opposite sex could not accomplish. But the nature of their gender will bring a different nuance in how that job is accomplished. And there

---

[112] CF Andreades, S. (2018). EnGendered: God's gift of gender difference in relationship. Bellingham, WA: Lexham Press.

will naturally be jobs that tend to line up better with the masculine or the feminine design given by God.

I have seen this in my marriage with Abby. We don't line up in all the traditional ways men or women might. Abby is way better at accounting and home repair. I am way better at cooking and cleaning. But Abby's powerful nurturing ability, her creative flair, her incredible relational intuition, her amazing ability to remember and accomplish a gazillion tasks at once are all such a huge blessing to me.

And I know she feels safe and flourishes under my leadership. I see this as I work hard to pray and plan how God would lead us as a couple. I see it as I give myself to listening to Abby, counseling her, receiving and implementing her counsel. I see it as I make time for us to pray together and dig into God's word. I see it when I cherish her and communicate my love for her through cards, regular dates, physical affection, and compliments. It is amazing just how far my encouragement can go with my wife. There was many a time in her musical career that my feedback kept her going when she felt like giving up.

I am so grateful for 40 years of loving each other and enjoying some of the mystery of imaging the diversity, unity, and love of our Triune God!

Thursday, September 15

I wanted to reflect a little more on sexuality and life. I think a lot of people who grew up around the time I did have a hard time understanding biblical sexual ethics. When I was young, most of the stereotypes of Christians depicted them as puritanical, legalistic, uptight, and into body shaming. We thought Christians were pretty ridiculous on this issue.

I later found out that most of this was unfounded. Christians tended to be pretty open about sex, and most married Christians seemed to be pretty intentional in pursuing growth and enjoyment in romance and sex. I later found lots of really good books that celebrated and supported married sex.[113] I was shocked to learn that there is a whole book of the Bible dedicated to the romantic, erotic experience of a married couple.[114]

But I also had to wrestle with the pretty narrow sexual ethic taught in the Bible. I didn't get it at first. I didn't understand why two people of the same sex couldn't be married.[115] I didn't understand why unmarried people couldn't experiment together with sex. I didn't understand why people had to wait to be married to have sex.[116] I didn't get why solo sex was

---

[113] Wheat, E. & Wheat, G. (2010). Intended for pleasure: sex technique and sexual fulfillment in Christian marriage. Grand Rapids, MI: Revell. Or Piper, J. & Taylor, J. (2005). Sex and the supremacy of Christ. Wheaton, Ill: Crossway Books or Mahaney, C. (2018). Sex, romance, and the glory of God: what every Christian husband needs to know / C. J. Mahaney. Wheaton, Illinois: Crossway.

[114] Song of Solomon

[115] Leviticus 20:13, 1 Corinthians 6:9

[116] Deut 22:23-29, 1 Corinthians 6:12-20 – sexual immorality (Greek: porneia) is any sexual relations outside of marriage.

discouraged.[117] I was tripped up by my presuppositions on gender or sexual fluidity, the place of pleasure, individualism, and humanism.

What helped me was to see that sex was created by God with a certain purpose. It is wrapped into what it means to be human as a man or a woman. It is something that is at the core of our identity as men or women. And to deviate from God's design is an insult against the image of God in us both individually and in relationships. Our bodies are not meant to be our own. They belong to God, and to some degree, to each other. Our bodies are to be used according to God's purposes and for blessing others. My body is not primarily nor foremost for my pleasure. My sexuality is not my choice. Our sexuality is not primarily about

---

[117] While solo sex or masturbation is not explicitly named as a sexual sin, it is not in line with God's design for our sex drives – as something meant to create appropriate community in compliment with the opposite sex. Sexual pleasure and orgasm are designed for covenantal intimacy in marriage, outside of marriage, erotic energy should be directed toward a healthy community experience, anticipation and enjoyment of communion with God, and a devotion to masculine or feminine service. Masturbation will work contrary to this pursuit. Often, masturbation is a false substitute for healthy relationships. Learning to abstain from solo sex and to use sexual energy to build communion with God and healthy community is key. CF: "Erotic energy is meant for another person, in love. If you are a woman, then it is meant for a man, and vice versa. Masturbation turns this erotic energy in on oneself. A person becomes sexually cross-eyed. What is meant for another person, in love, has been turned to the gratification of oneself. Masturbation, therefore, is a symbol of loneliness, not love. One way to overcome it, besides controlling what you read and watch, is to begin to foster genuine friendship with others." Percy, A. (2006). Theology of the Body Made Simple (p. 79). Boston, MA: Pauline Books & Media

our own satisfaction or being true to ourselves, but about God and others.[118] Our sexual behavior will have a strong effect on our relationship with God and with others. The Bible says that sexual sin is a deep sin against the body as created by God.[119]

Therefore, reserving sexual activity for marriage is a fulfillment of God's design. And this sort of purity brings with it a freedom from damage to ourselves and our relationship with others. It is very clear in scripture that purity brings greater intimacy with God and greater availability to be useful to others.

---

[118] Consider 1 Corinthians 6:12-20: "You say, "I am allowed to do anything" – but not everything is good for you. And even though "I am allowed to do anything," I must not become a slave to anything. You say, "Food was made for the stomach, and the stomach for food." (This is true, though someday God will do away with both of them.) But you can't say that our bodies were made for sexual immorality. They were made for the Lord, and the Lord cares about our bodies. And God will raise us from the dead by his power, just as he raised our Lord from the dead. Don't you realize that your bodies are actually parts of Christ? Should a man take his body, which is part of Christ, and join it to a prostitute? Never! And don't you realize that if a man joins himself to a prostitute, he becomes one body with her? For the Scriptures say, "The two are united into one." But the person who is joined to the Lord is one spirit with him. Run from sexual sin! No other sin so clearly affects the body as this one does. For sexual immorality is a sin against your own body. Don't you realize that your body is the temple of the Holy Spirit, who lives in you and was given to you by God? You do not belong to yourself, for God bought you with a high price. So, you must honor God with your body." (1 Corinthians 6:12–20) Also, for further study see "The Rise and Triumph of the Modern Self." Carl Trueman.

[119] "Run from sexual sin! No other sin so clearly affects the body as this one does. For sexual immorality is a sin against your own body." (1 Corinthians 6:18)

[120] Even the mainstream culture has seen the benefit of sexual self-control amidst the rampant sexual experimentation and indulgence in pornography that has brought so much harm. [121]

This understanding of sexuality is powerful enough to change the mind, heart, and behavior of someone, like me, committed to a very different approach. It also has transformed countless cultures committed to very different sexual ethics. It

---

[120] "God blesses those whose hearts are pure, for they will see God." (Matthew 5:8)

"In a wealthy home some utensils are made of gold and silver, and some are made of wood and clay. The expensive utensils are used for special occasions, and the cheap ones are for everyday use. If you keep yourself pure, you will be a special utensil for honorable use. Your life will be clean, and you will be ready for the Master to use you for every good work. Run from anything that stimulates youthful lusts. Instead, pursue righteous living, faithfulness, love, and peace. Enjoy the companionship of those who call on the Lord with pure hearts." (2 Timothy 2:20–22)

"Work at living in peace with everyone, and work at living a holy life, for those who are not holy will not see the Lord." (Hebrews 12:14)

"You were cleansed from your sins when you obeyed the truth, so now you must show sincere love to each other as brothers and sisters. Love each other deeply with all your heart." (1 Peter 1:22)

[121] E.G.: a) The No-Fap movement, see https://en.wikipedia.org/wiki/NoFap , b) Escaping Porn Addiction, https://www.ted.com/talks/eli_nash_escaping_porn_addiction c) Make Love Not Porn, Cindy Gallop, https://www.ted.com/talks/cindy_gallop_make_love_not_porn.

was powerful enough to transform the ancient Greco-Roman culture that was awash in sexual promiscuity.[122]

Friday, September 16

When I first encountered biblical teaching on sexuality, I wondered how it would apply to being single. It seemed, at first, that if a man or woman was not able to be in a heterosexual monogamous marriage, he or she was missing out on God's design in creation. The only other option outside of marriage, in my view, was a second-class existence of reluctantly being single and celibate. That was a really difficult prospect for me at the time. I am so grateful for my friend Ryan's counsel and all the good resources that help expound the biblical teaching in this area.[123]

Ultimately, the pleasure of sex is meant to promote the enjoyment and deepening of union between a husband and wife and point married and unmarried people to the greater and eternal enjoyment of the deepest union we can have, that between God and his people. The abstinence of the single person

---

[122] Kevin DeYoung, The First Sexual Revolution: The Triumph of Christian Morality in the Roman Empire, The Gospel Coalition, September 9, 2019, https://www.thegospelcoalition.org/blogs/kevin-deyoung/first-sexual-revolution-triumph-christian-morality-roman-empire/

[123] Like See Karol Józef Wojtyła, Theology of the Body, Rome, 1997 or its introduction: Christopher West, Theology of the Body for Beginners: A Basic Introduction to Pope John Paul II's Sexual Revolution (West Chester, PA: Ascension, 2004). Another resource in this line: Nancy R. Pearcey, Love Thy Body: Answering Hard Questions about Life and Sexuality (Grand Rapids, MI: Baker, 2018).

can serve to increase their communion with God, their involvement with community and their anticipation of the fulfillment of their sexuality in ultimate pleasurable and deep union with God.[124] This gift, properly understood and used, is meant to show us just how wonderful and glorious it is to belong to God

---

[124] Consider Psalm 16:11, (ESV): "You make known to me the path of life; in your presence there is fullness of joy; at your right hand are pleasures forevermore."

1 Corinthians 7:32–35: "I want you to be free from the concerns of this life. An unmarried man can spend his time doing the Lord's work and thinking how to please him. But a married man has to think about his earthly responsibilities and how to please his wife. His interests are divided. In the same way, a woman who is no longer married or has never been married can be devoted to the Lord and holy in body and in spirit. But a married woman has to think about her earthly responsibilities and how to please her husband. I am saying this for your benefit, not to place restrictions on you. I want you to do whatever will help you serve the Lord best, with as few distractions as possible."

Ephesians 5:32: "This is a great mystery, but it is an illustration of the way Christ and the church are one."

Revelation 21:2–5a: "And I saw the holy city, the new Jerusalem, coming down from God out of heaven like a bride beautifully dressed for her husband. I heard a loud shout from the throne, saying, "Look, God's home is now among his people! He will live with them, and they will be his people. God himself will be with them. He will wipe every tear from their eyes, and there will be no more death or sorrow or crying or pain. All these things are gone forever." And the one sitting on the throne said, "Look, I am making everything new!"

and therefore to enjoy a indescribably glorious union with him through Christ.

First, it is really clear in the Bible that singleness is not a second-class existence. Although God has created mankind to complement one another as male and female, and although marriage is the more common state, and although sexual relations are considered holy and good when used according to God's design, singleness is no less important in being human together. It can even be argued that it is preferable to being married.[125]

In the new creation, all redeemed humanity will be single. There will be no more marriage as we have known it. We will not engage in sexual relations. But we will all experience the fullness of what earthly marriage and sexual relations signified. We will experience the full reality of being spiritually united in Christ in a deep eternal, pleasurable and holy union with all our

---

[125] 1 Corinthians 7:32–35: [32] I want you to be free from the concerns of this life. An unmarried man can spend his time doing the Lord's work and thinking how to please him. [33] But a married man has to think about his earthly responsibilities and how to please his wife. [34] His interests are divided. In the same way, a woman who is no longer married or has never been married can be devoted to the Lord and holy in body and in spirit. But a married woman has to think about her earthly responsibilities and how to please her husband. [35] I am saying this for your benefit, not to place restrictions on you. I want you to do whatever will help you serve the Lord best, with as few distractions as possible.

God-given differences.[126] We will be as brothers and sisters in a family. So, singleness lives in and for the ultimate union of Christ and his church.

Singleness allows greater devotion to the ultimate union. Singles are able to be undistracted with the need to prioritize a marriage and a biological family. They can give themselves more fully to the progress of the Kingdom of Heaven. They can benefit from a greater focus on prayer and communion with God as well as significant ministry to others. When properly understood and practiced, singleness can be a tremendous benefit to the life and mission of the church. Many churches have formed deep community and effective mission through banding singles together into subgroups for discipleship, networking and community. Other churches have encouraged their singles to connect with a Christian Order that

---

[126] Consider Psalm 16:11, (ESV): "You make known to me the path of life; in your presence there is fullness of joy; at your right hand are pleasures forevermore."

Ephesians 5:32: "This is a great mystery, but it is an illustration of the way Christ and the church are one."

Revelation 21:2–5a: "And I saw the holy city, the new Jerusalem, coming down from God out of heaven like a bride beautifully dressed for her husband. I heard a loud shout from the throne, saying, "Look, God's home is now among his people! He will live with them, and they will be his people. God himself will be with them. He will wipe every tear from their eyes, and there will be no more death or sorrow or crying or pain. All these things are gone forever." And the one sitting on the throne said, "Look, I am making everything new!"

helps form and foster community, mission and support among singles.[127] I am so grateful for the vibrancy of celibacy in the church in my day.

Of course, this service to the church is as a man or a woman. Singles are not sexually neutered. Being unmarried does not deprive us of opportunities to live out our femininity if a woman or our masculinity if a man. Sisters in a family remain women. Brothers in a family remain men. As women or men, they will live and love in that family according to their God-given gender. More on this tomorrow.

Saturday, September 17

I have seen this work out in my church and other churches over many years. When we walk together as men and women in Christ, seeking to let his word hold sway and relying on his power and grace, we are able to live in ways that appropriately express God's design in gender. It is really sweet when this happens.

It is no wonder that it has been common sense for centuries. In a healthy church or family, it is natural and biblical for brothers to take the initiative to lead, provide for and protect their sisters as men should. It would be appropriate for them to provide direction, counsel, and encouragement for their sisters. It is natural for them to guard and ensure the interests and priorities of the family.

---

[127] Compare with "For the Body," Tim Tennant

It is natural for sisters to provide vital counsel and insight to sharpen their brothers' leadership in these priorities and interests. It is appropriate for brothers to allow their sisters to also take a degree of initiative and leadership in various ways without fear or pride keeping them from sharing power. It would be appropriate for sisters to be bold in leading even while respecting, supporting, and appreciating the God-given strengths and call of their brothers in providing masculine leadership for the family.

It is natural for sisters to fill out the details and structures under the interests and priorities stewarded by their brothers. It would be appropriate for sisters to use their relational skills and intuition to nurture and promote the unity of the family. It is appropriate for sisters to receive their brothers' encouragement and, in turn, be vital assistants in the life and mission of the family.

In the church, brothers and sisters can operate alongside one another in complementary and appropriate ways to further the life and mission of the church. As they do so, they retain core aspects that are the result of the clear spiritual, relational, psychological, vocational, and biological distinctiveness of men and women as designed by God. This is true whether relating as husband and wife in marriage or as brothers and sisters in a church community. Thank God, he has made us men and women, and we will always retain this and live it out as a good thing, whether single or married! Thank God for the ultimate family of the church, where we can live out vital community as women and men without shame and for the glory of God.

Sunday, September 18 –

Hope this liturgy blesses married couples today!

A Liturgy for Husband & Wife at Close of Day[128]

Husband: *At* death, we will part.

Wife: *Therefore*, let us not take the blessing of our life together for granted.

(*Silence* is kept as both spouses consider for a moment the gravity of this truth.)

Husband: *May our hearts be ever drawn towards You, O Lord In* whose three-personed perfection of love burns the fire that would kindle also our two-personed imperfection into a oneness that is warmed and forged of your holy flames,

Wife: *A* thing that is both an echo and seed and a play upon a stage, portraying the promise of union with Christ that is to come.

Together: *We are unworthy players, O Lord, unworthy to portray your glory.*
We are weak. We are jealous. We are easily wounded.
We are petty. We are embittered. We store up remembrances of wounds.

---

[128] A Liturgy for a Husband & Wife at Close of Day, Douglas McKelvey, Every Moment Holy, Rabbit Room Press (2017), p 147

We are insecure.
We hurt one another.
We do not deal with our conflicts well.
We fail to love as you have loved.
Forgive us even the failures of this day.

(*Silence* is kept. If either husband or wife has need to make amends, they may do so now.)

Husband: *I* am not strong enough in my own strength to be husband to you.

Wife: *And* I am not strong enough in my own strength to be wife to you.

Together: *Let* us turn to God together then, asking the strength that we need.

(*Husband* and wife take hands.)

Together: *Give* us therefore the strength that comes from the grace that flows from your heart alone, O God, that we might live and move and breathe in air of that grace, receiving it in ourselves, and then offering it daily to one another. Without grace, our marriage will wither as a vine unrooted. But sustained by your grace, it will ever flourish and bloom and flower and fruit.

Husband: *Forgive* us our failures and our sins against one another and against our marriage, O God, and restore now our hearts to you and to one another.

Wife: *Repair* the damages of our selfishness, our thoughtlessness, our inconsistencies. Draw us again together at the close of this day, in love, and forgiveness, and fellowship and peace.

Together: *May* we sleep this night side by side in unity of heart and mind and purpose. May we wake in the morning in solidarity and delight, thankful for the sharing of this life, for the companion who journeys beside us, for hands to hold and arms to embrace, and lips to kiss at the close of day.

Husband: *May* we love one another more at the end of this day than we did at its beginning.

Wife: *May* we treasure one another more at the end of this week than we did at its start.

Husband: *May* we hold one another as more precious, more respected, more dear at the shuttering of this month, than we did at its opening.

Wife: *May* we delight in our companionship and take heart in the sharing of our burdens more at the close of this year, than we did as it opened

Husband: *May* we reflect your glory far more fully in the beauty of our shared relationship at the hour we are parted by death than we did even in the hour of our wedding.

Together: *Bless* our marriage. Kindle our desire. Teach us to be friends and lovers and companions and may this our marriage exist not only for our benefit but may the bond between us grow to be a shelter and a blessing for others as well.

Husband: *We* ask these things in the name of the Father, and of the Son, and of the Holy Spirit.

Wife: *Amen.*

Together: *And* now, with joined hearts, together we bring to you these burdens of our day.

(*Husband* and wife may now freely petition their heavenly Father with all worries, burdens and concerns.)

Chapter 7: O Church Arise!

Monday, September 19

This week I want to focus on all that has gone on in and through the Church in my lifetime. It truly has been a golden age where so many of the promises for the Church have been substantially fulfilled. We never would have dreamed that one lifetime would see the good news of Christ going to each and every ethnic group in the world. We never would have envisioned vital, loving, Bible-saturated churches in every village throughout the world. The true Church has always prayed for the great harvest of the Jews to take place, we got to see it. And many churches throughout the ages have taught and prayed in line with Ephesians 4 that the Church would be fully mature, a powerful reflection of the fullness of Christ and his love. The 21st Century saw this fulfilled beyond anything we have seen before. Truly we have been like those who are dreaming, as Psalm 126 says.

> *"When the LORD brought back his exiles to Jerusalem, it was like a dream! We were filled with laughter, and we sang for joy. And the other nations said, "What amazing things the LORD has done for them." Yes, the LORD has done amazing things for us! What joy!"*[129]

Ultimately, it was God's grace and mercy alone that brought all these things about. And it all happened like a phoenix from the fire. The political and economic upheavals of the early 21st

---

[129] Psalm 126:1-3

century were the fire, the reconciliation of the Church and then the various councils and the many blessings that followed were the phoenix and its victorious flight. So, let me talk a little more about the great reconciliation.

Disunity has troubled the Church for the past 1,000 years. There were various reasons for disunity, they included deviations from biblical faithfulness, the unbiblical practice of entangling church and state, disagreements on the nature and practice of the unity of the church, as well as misunderstanding the importance of freedom of conscience and inquiry. These disagreements could be deadly and even cataclysmic. The eastern church had already split with the western church through mutual excommunications in 1054. This split contributed to the abuse, slaughter, and war crimes of the Crusades. The Protestant Reformation and split from the Roman Catholic Church was initiated in 1521 with the excommunication of Martin Luther. This split led to much bloodshed in Europe and centuries of religious cynicism in the West. These splits are a great blot on the reputation of Christ's church. But the bridegroom did not abandon his errant bride.

After the fall of the West as we knew it, it seemed God put it in the hearts of thousands of church leaders at once to gather for a great council, not seen since the early councils of the church, such as that at Nicea. The Pope and Cardinals of the Roman Catholic Church all simultaneously requested such a council, the Patriarch and bishops of Eastern Orthodoxy had the same inspiration. Leaders in the Protestant Church among Lutherans, Anglicans, Presbyterians, Congregationalists, Baptists, Methodists, Pentecostals and Independents all found themselves simultaneously having the strong inclination to meet together with the whole church for a grand council. It truly was an amazing work of the Holy Spirit.

So, they commenced their Council in earnest. They weren't even sure of how to proceed beyond gathering together in Christ's name and praying. That's how it started, a month of fasting and prayer before the actual meeting, and then two weeks of prayer, worship in song and confession of sin together. The presence of the Lord was so powerful that many delegates said they could not have lasted more than two weeks in such conviction and renewal because the power of the Lord had such a profound effect on soul and body.

Their next work was to define what Christ was calling them to receive and do. They knew right away that Christ's calling was the reality and necessity of the profound unity in Christ that was to be worked out in tangible and effective ways. Defining and delineating this call was to take them a whole year of hard work, with multiple recesses in their meetings and a massive tempest of activity of hundreds of committees tasked with various aspects of this move towards unity.

It is all well-documented but let me summarize the results. First, they grounded the Church's unity in the actual and profound unity all believers have in Christ himself. Any and all visible aspects of unity flow out of our union in Christ, through faith in the good news of Christ. Second, they recognized the word of God as ultimately authoritative over the Church while affirming that the Church is necessary for the word's proper understanding and practice. Third, they clarified and resolved historic disagreements on the Trinity and justification.

They clarified that the Holy Spirit proceeded from the Father through the Son, not from the Father and the Son in the same manner. They clarified that justification is comprised of two aspects, imputation and vindication. Justification through imputation is through faith alone by grace alone by Christ alone received at the moment of genuine faith and repentance. Justification through vindication is through the verification at the final judgment of Christ-like fruit in keeping with genuine faith and repentance. These core issues were settled by this council, a truly amazing result, more than a thousand years in the waiting. We had to pinch ourselves to make sure we weren't just dreaming. I'll cover some more of the results throughout this week.

Tuesday, September 20

Settling the key disagreements that had divided the church was a first step in unity. The next steps involved defining the nature, authority and structure of the whole church under this new understanding and call to unity. This required just as much work. O, how helpful were the results!

First, they defined the nature of the church as the union of all the faithful across all time, regardless of denomination or disagreements on secondary issues. Faithfulness was defined as sincere belief and obedience to the faith as put forth in scripture and defined by the first four ecumenical councils.[130] The

---

[130] These are the First Council of Nicea (325), First Council of Constantinople (381), Council of Ephesus (431) and the Council of Chalcedon (451).

Council on Church Unity supplied this summary of this faithfulness as follows:

- *Faith in the Trinity, One in Being, Three in Persons*
- *Faith in the Father, the Source of All*
- *Faith in the Son, eternally begotten, fully God having become fully man, as Jesus Christ, to be the Only Savior and King of Kings.*
- *Faith in the Holy Spirit, proceeding from the Father through the Son, the Giver of Life*
- *Faith in the Word of God as Inspired and Authoritative, according to the teaching of the Apostles.*
- *Faith in the Whole Church – the People of God, the Body of Christ himself and the Buttress of Truth*

The Council on Church Unity also clarified the authority of the church. This had been an area of disagreement – largely through misunderstanding. They stated that the authority of the Church comes from Christ alone and does not exist apart from Christ's rightful authority. This authority is exercised first by the word of Christ, the scriptures as recognized and received by the Church, including the 39 books of the Old Testament and the 27 books of the New Testament. The seven books of the apocrypha are understood as helpful but not authoritative. Christ also exercises his authority through the teaching and official decisions of the officers of the church in communion with the whole Church.[131] The exercise of the authority of the

---

[131] Consider Matthew 18:15-20: [15] "If another believer sins against you, go privately and point out the offense. If the other person listens and confesses it, you have won that person back. [16] But if you are unsuccessful, take one or two others with you and go back again, so that everything you say

Church is important and necessary, but always submitted to the authority of the word of God. Where the Church as a whole can determine that any portion of the Church had failed to submit to scripture, such teachings and decisions can be negated. These understandings brought great unity to the Church. The Council on Church Unity was able to work through many details and many past teachings to arrive at extensive agreement that helped them delineate many positions and present a unified Book of Common Worship for use by individuals and local parishes. The Council allowed many non-essential distinctives to remain among various associations of churches, but these associations nevertheless acted in sincere unity with the whole church under the leadership of the Council on Church Unity.

The Book of Common Worship devoted a section to the structure of the Church. They recognized two officers of the church, elders and deacons. These officers are selected according to biblical qualifications and affirmed by a vote of the church they serve. Membership in the church is by a profession of faith and baptism, as received by the church officers and an affirmation of the local parish. All such churches are joined in districts where churches and leaders come together for mutual support, shared mission and accountability, the officers of churches in a

---

may be confirmed by two or three witnesses. [17] If the person still refuses to listen, take your case to the church. Then if he or she won't accept the church's decision, treat that person as a pagan or a corrupt tax collector. [18] "I tell you the truth, whatever you forbid on earth will be forbidden in heaven, and whatever you permit on earth will be permitted in heaven. [19] "I also tell you this: If two of you agree here on earth concerning anything you ask, my Father in heaven will do it for you. [20] For where two or three gather together as my followers, I am there among them." (Matthew 18:15–20)

district elect delegates to oversee their joint activities and commitments. These delegates are called district bishops but do not exercise any independent authority from the church officers. These delegates then can elect further delegates who oversee various levels of structures within the whole church – variously designated as bishops of their level. All such delegates must be officers in local parishes. These levels of structure exist at five total levels going from districts to sections, to regions, provinces and finally, the ecumenical council. The ecumenical council is made up of delegates from the provinces along with various experts who serve its committees. It is overseen by a chief delegate, designated as the prime bishop, who is elected for a five-year term. He holds no independent authority but is very influential as he directs the work of the ecumenical council. Authority is understood as originating from Christ, exercised by local churches and expressed in the various levels of organization flowing from the union of local churches. I won't get into all the details, but this structure along with the Book of Common Worship and Council Statements had a profound effect on the health and success of the whole Church.

Wednesday, September 21

All this amazing change was a catalyst for what followed – an extended time of great prosperity for the life and mission of the whole Church and its positive and powerful influence on every aspect of human endeavors. It seemed the greatest extent of the Kingdom of God on earth ever in history. It was as if God answered the prayers of thousands of years of believers who cried out for his Kingdom to come and his will to be done. Certainly, no one would say it paralleled the future kingdom that awaits us after Christ's return, but it was nevertheless a miracle to behold and experience.

As the influence of the various Church Councils were felt along with the pervasive positive influence of billions of believers the whole world was affected. The Church left its mark on philosophy, theology, ethics, education, literature, media, the arts, poetry, science, technology, economics, business, politics, architecture, fashion, beauty, entertainment and sports. It did so without coercion or discord, but through the voluntary acceptance of its teaching and example by the majority of numerous cultures. I could spend a lot of time giving examples of this, in addition to the ones I've already described. Let me cite just a few examples.

First, architecture flourished in this golden age of the Church. The architectural guild that was created was a powerful force in addressing key issues in architecture. The trends in merely utilitarian architecture, often lacking in aesthetic and social value, were better controlled. The guild created codes for architecture that required appropriate elements of aesthetic and social value in every construction project. Major buildings, ones that by virtue of their scale would necessarily become landmarks, were required to provide significant aesthetic and social value. Often such projects involved a cooperative effort of private owners, local communities, various guilds and unions and even federal government. This resulted in many amazing structures that combined features that were truly beautiful to behold but also created a sense of space that benefited the occupants and the community far beyond their utilitarian aspects.

I think of the campus of St. Augustine University, built amidst the city of Naples, Florida, with its balconies, fountains, shopping centers, small business offices and laboratories, artist shoppes and museums, magnificent ocean-side dormitories, housing units, multiple gardens, groves and playgrounds. It is truly a glorious place to visit and experience. I have a few friends who live there and really love it. It is a shining example of good architecture and the power of the cooperative efforts of the architectural guild, educational organizations, local government, science and art guilds and the Church. It presents a living display of what it looks like when the true, good and beautiful are working in harmony.

I will journal about the next two examples tomorrow. They are fashion and sports. I hope it will be helpful!

Thursday, September 22

Two more examples to share today. Hope they help you! Secondly, this golden age brought about some wonderful changes in fashion and beauty. The various regional fashion guilds came up with many influential fashion innovations. Most of the guilds were influenced by a Christian view of beauty and the body, a view that had been well-described by Pope John Paul's Theology of the Body.[132] This view is one where the beauty of the

---

[132] See Karol Józef Wojtyła, Theology of the Body, Rome, 1997 or its introduction: Christopher West, Theology of the Body for Beginners: A Basic Introduction to Pope John Paul II's Sexual Revolution (West Chester, PA: Ascension, 2004). Another resource in this line: Nancy R. Pearcey, Love Thy Body: Answering Hard Questions about Life and Sexuality (Grand Rapids, MI: Baker, 2018).

human body, either male or female, is celebrated without abusing the whole image of God shown both through body and soul. The historic problem with fashion was the tendency to either see the body as something to be covered and hidden or to display the body in a narrow, sexualized way. We could describe these poles as body-shaming and body-defaming. The fashion guilds led us onto a path of celebrating and respecting the human body and soul through a diversity of beautiful and functional fashions. They were not squeamish about the nude human form, clearly declared "very good" by God, yet they understood that the clothed body is the ultimate adornment we find for humanity in scripture.[133] Additionally, they taught that appropriate clothing can provide protection from the elements, greater functionality for various tasks, ways to identify oneself fittingly, opportunities for human creativity and a degree of protection from sexual lust, objectification and mistreatment in this broken world.

Women's fashions trended towards elegant dresses, blouses and skirts, while retaining comfortable and functional casual and athletic wear. Fashions were more discreet yet still adequately accented the beauty of the feminine body. Various accessories that highlighted the face and neck became more popular, hats, headbands, tiaras, barrettes, combs, beads and hairpins were used in many attractive and innovative ways.

---

[133] See Genesis 1:31, 3:21, 41:42, Leviticus 8:13, Job 29:14, Psalm 104:1-2, Matthew 25:36, Mark 5:15, 9:2-3, 2 Corinthians 5:4, Revelation 7:9, 19:8 CF: Illumination and Investiture: The Royal Significance of the Tree of Wisdom in Genesis 3, William Wilder, WTJ 68 (2006): 51-69

Necklaces became common, ranging from simple cloths and knots to pearls and diamonds.

Men's fashions, similarly, highlighted masculine features while remaining comfortable and functional. It became more common for men to dress up a bit more outside of casual contexts. Formalwear became common for special occasions. Sports coats, nice pants and shoes were more commonly seen in the workplace, the marketplace and in church. All around, a healthy fashion-consciousness and greater intention in celebrating the beauty of humanity elevated the whole arena of fashion.

Third, and final example to mention is sports. First, it was the desire of every sports league to make schedule changes that were more supportive of family and church life. No more than two games per week were scheduled by any sports – from professional all the way down to little kids' leagues. Sundays were no longer a sports day but a day of rest for all of society. Although many of us missed having football, baseball and golf on Sundays, it was worth it. As a result, on Sundays it seemed that the whole world settled into a day of rest and refreshment, an oasis of renewing the wonder of resting in God's good creation. Many attended worship services, most visited with friends and families, many took walks as groups. It was so nice to be out in the neighborhoods strolling and interacting with neighbors. Many also made Sundays a time to visit and take gifts to the poor and lonely in their parishes.

The nature of sports changed somewhat, too. It was less a consuming passion and more an opportunity for exercise, teamwork and recreation. There was less attention paid to professional athletes and more attention paid to healthy participation in local sports clubs of various types setup for the health and thriving of communities. It seemed that everybody spent a few hours every week in some sort of group sports activity through a local club. There was a trend away from vicarious sports experiences experienced from the comfort of your couch towards active participation experienced as part of a local club or team, alongside your neighbors and friends.

Well, I hope these additional specific examples help you see some of the benefits that the unity and health of the Church brought to humanity. I could give similar examples in all the arenas, but I hope this is enough for you to imagine how things were. It really was a wonderful time to be alive.

Friday, September 23

I need to mention the effect the health of the Church had on the mission of the church in terms of spreading the good news of Christ and growing the Church worldwide. At the beginning of the 21st Century there were about 2 billion people of a total population of 6 billion world-wide who identified as Christian. There were about 7,500 of the 17,440 total people groups who had no viable witness of Christ in their midst. Only 100,000 of the total world Jewish population of 13 million believed in Jesus of Nazareth as the Messiah. Within 50 years, all these numbers changed radically.

At the micro level, what happened was that the health of local churches and the reputation of local Christians increased so much that churches that used to represent 1-10% of the local population suddenly found themselves doubling every year.

This led to multiplication of parishes to the point of a local church for each village or neighborhood in a city. Attendance in some places reached near 100% of the population.

Regions of the world with little or no Christian presence experienced special attention from the broader Christian world. Missionary efforts alongside educational and economic development, brought in a way respectful of the current culture, led to new and rapidly growing churches in previously resistant areas of the world such as Pakistan, Afghanistan, Northern Africa, Southern Asia and former communist countries. Areas previously shut off to Christians under Muslim rule opened up and many came to Christ. There was tremendous growth of the churches in these areas. Amazingly, they grew while remaining respectful of non-Christians and much of the Muslim culture and while experiencing much favor and respect from Muslim authorities themselves. God seemed to give hundreds of millions of Muslims powerful dreams that revealed the validity of the followers of Isa al-Masih (Jesus.) This led to much sincere inquiry into the Christian scriptures by whole extended family groups and even whole mosques.

Also, areas previously under the influence of post-Christian secularism experienced massive renewal. Europe and North America became vibrant examples of devout and healthy Christian influence that remained respectful and socially inclusive of those with different worldviews. The churches in these areas experienced powerful renewal and explosive growth.

Perhaps most amazingly, the faith of the Jewish people was dramatically changed. This was due in part to the work of repentance and renewal in the Church. The Council on Church

Unity made numerous overtures to the world Jewish population to express deep remorse and regret over the previous treatment of Jewish people throughout history. They identified the gross contradiction of following a Jewish Jesus while persecuting his Jewish brethren. Additionally, the genuine love and respect towards the Jewish people that pervaded the renewed and reunited Church alongside the Church's vibrant witness had a profound effect on many Jews. The wise and vigorous work of many Messianic Jews as part of the larger church resulted in an exponential increase in Messianic Jews. At first it was a trickle, then a stream, then a river, then a massive torrent of conversions. By the middle of the century, it seemed it was considered most Jewish to have received Yeshua HaMashiach as Lord and Savior.[134] From what we could tell, every person of Jewish heritage became a believer in Jesus.

All this amazing fruitfulness seemed to indicate the return of Christ would come at any moment. It was then, when it seemed nothing could go wrong, that the outrageous claims of the Messengers emerged, and everything began to change. Even so, we remain deeply grateful for the indescribable golden age we experienced.

---

[134] Romans 11:12,15 "Now if the Gentiles were enriched because the people of Israel turned down God's offer of salvation, think how much greater a blessing the world will share when they finally accept it... For since their rejection meant that God offered salvation to the rest of the world, their acceptance will be even more wonderful. It will be life for those who were dead!"

Saturday, September 24

Another aspect of the golden age I want to talk about is the effect on vocation. It seems that for centuries many Christians believed that if you really wanted to serve God you needed to work full time for the church or a Christian agency or missions organization. Often people understood other employment as secular and almost a necessary evil to provide income to fund holier endeavors. This golden age dramatically altered this. The Council on Church & State helped define some key truths that altered that historic and mistaken perspective.

They addressed the history of the secular -sacred divide. This perspective is more of the result of ancient Greek thought than biblical truth. Beginning with Plato and continuing through some of the thought of much respected theologians like Augustine, Aquinas and Luther and others, sacred and secular have been seen as distinct levels of existence. The spiritual was seen as superior to the physical. Church service was seen as superior to farming or even parenting. The soul was seen as superior to the body. But none of these ideas are found in scripture.

A robust doctrine of creation was reestablished by the Council on Humankind. The soul and the body were identified as cocreated and united in humanity as the image of God. Both operated together to image God. The body along with all the physical aspects of creation were established as integral and necessary means of displaying the character and qualities of the invisible God. The soul was designed to have a body and the body a soul. Thus, all occupations in line with God's moral law were equally worshipful. The fall of mankind into sin didn't negate this reality, only caused all endeavors to be tainted by sin, whether designated secular or sacred, they all were meant to be truly sacred.

So, the hierarchy of importance of work, of vocation, was eliminated and replaced with a dignity for all vocation as the proper imaging of God in creation. Whether sharing the good news of Christ and ministering the sacraments or trading on the stock market or digging ditches, all was meant to be worship of God.

Of course, grasping this truth shifted many things. Vocations that previously were less valued became important. Ditch diggers were better paid and respected. Stockbrokers felt less guilty and enjoyed being generous. Pastors and church workers moved into other fields of work without feeling they had missed their call. More people volunteered to help in church life and mission roles, no longer feeling that only especially "holy" men and women could do that. The sense of the sacred became more pervasive in many occupations and there was a sense of the divine in so many tasks previously considered mundane. Truly, all types of work became greatly dignified with these changes, even lawyers!

Sunday, September 25

(BTW: tomorrow is my birthday!) Well, I hope this weeks' worth of journaling has been helpful to you. I want to finish with a Sunday liturgy on the church. It is a favorite hymn of mine from Timothy Dwight, *I Love Thy Kingdom, Lord*.

I love Thy kingdom, Lord,
The house of Thine abode,

The Church our blest Redeemer bought
With His own precious blood.

I love the Church, O God!
Her walls before Thee stand,
Dear as the apple of Thine eye
And graven on Thy hand.

For her my tears shall fall,
For her my prayers ascend;
To her my cares and toils be given
Till toils and cares shall end.

Beyond my highest joy
I prize her heavenly ways,
Her sweet communion, solemn vows,
Her hymns of love and praise.

Sure as Thy truth shall last,
To Zion shall be given
The brightest glories earth can yield,
And brighter bliss of heaven.

Chapter 8: We Are Family

Monday, September 26

I had a wonderful birthday visit yesterday with Abby and Zoey and Arman and their 6 children, Aafreen, Zana, Soroush, Farzad, Ervin and Saphia. They range from 14 to 2. They are so beautiful – a mix of at least six different ethnicities. They are so precious to us. Being a grandparent has been one of the greatest joys of my life. (The rest of the gang would have come, too, but the prison only allows 10 visitors for special occasions.)

They brought me balloons and a birthday cake. It was so bittersweet. Their visit was both so joyful that I thought my heart would burst but so sorrowful that I thought my heart would break. I'm still recovering this morning from all the mixed emotions. Zoey's two oldest, both girls, Aafreen and Zana, were holding back tears much of the time. I asked Zana how she was feeling, and she burst into sobs. I hugged her and all she said, over and over, was "Grampa, please don't die, Grampa, please don't die." I told her that I love her very much and because of Jesus, we will never truly die. I reminded her of this promise for us first given to Mary of Bethany.[135] This is the power of hope – real hope, that overcomes this world, that overcomes death and evil. I barely got the words out but I'm so glad I did. I want her to know that there is something greater and longer lasting than this broken world.

---

[135] "Jesus told her, "I am the resurrection and the life. Anyone who believes in me will live, even after dying. Everyone who lives in me and believes in me will never ever die. Do you believe this, Martha?"" (John 11:25–26)

Farzad, the manly younger brother, was full more of anger than sadness. He told me that if anyone comes to get his mom and dad, he would fight them and escape. I so understand that testosterone-driven response. God has made men to be protectors and fighters for good. But left to itself, this response can grow hard and bitter. I hugged Farzad and told him that God will fight for us. But God wins by losing sometimes. Jesus let the bad men beat him, torture him and kill him so by his death he could overcome sin and hatred and evil. Farzad burst into tears. "But Grandpa, you're my best friend, you can't go now." That was a really hard moment. I held Farzad and cried with him. I told him I didn't want to go now. I loved being with him. But we have to trust Jesus to take care of us and bring us back together in time. I told him that would be the best party we've ever had, and we can do lots together and catch up on all that has gone on. He can tell me all the things he has learned about fishing and astronomy (his two favorite hobbies.)

Soroush seemed to be doing the best. He was sad but better able to trust God for his Grampa. He told me he was praying for me every morning and every night before he went to sleep. He told me he heard God tell him it was all gonna be okay. Soroush is our little prophet, full of faith and a close relationship with God. I told him to pray also for his sisters and brothers and his parents. The next months were gonna be hard and God will use his prayers to take care of everyone. He nodded his head with a tear in his eye. – O God, strengthen and keep this precious boy. Make him a source of strength to his siblings and his dear mom, who will struggle to deal with what is coming!

It was sweet to just hold and laugh with Ervin and Saphia. They are so cute and full of life. How precious life is! How beautiful are those created in the image of God! How amazing to watch children grow and interact with their world with such zest and wonder and innocence! My heart was both very full and very broken. I love them so much. I love Zoey and her wonderful, thoughtful and hard-working husband, Arman. O God, help me. Please carry this burden. Please remind me of your compassion – even amidst your sufferings. How you loved those around you. How you longed for them and their care even as you hung on the cross. How you loved your mother and the Apostle John, leaving instructions for your mother's care even as you were bearing the sins of the world.[136] O Savior, comfort me in my sorrow and this suffering!

Tuesday, September 27

I am gonna focus a little more on topics related to family this week. Maybe it is just therapy for me, but I hope there are some nuggets in here that will help you out.

Family is such a key part of life. So much revolves around family. It is where we first experience love and belonging. It is where we learn that we are not the center of the universe but connected to others who orbit around some center point together. We are both encouraged for gifts and goodness but also confronted with our selfishness and evil inside. Our first glimpses of the divine are often our mother and father – these God-like mighty figures who seem able to do anything but also

---

[136] See Luke 23:39-43 and John 19:25-27.

both love us and confront our waywardness. Family is such a significant thing in our lives.

It is so terribly wrong and sad that the experience of family is something that brings hurt and confusion for some. The forces at work in family are so powerful that they can strengthen us for the most difficult task or damage us, so we falter under the most routine tasks. This dual reality speaks to the importance of the family but also creates a longing for a family that stands above the frailty, imperfections and transience of our human family.

I certainly have not been a perfect husband and father. And I didn't grow up under perfect parents nor was I the perfect son. But, overall, I have been very blessed. I am very grateful for all I have been given by my family. My greatest struggle with my family is the temporal aspect. Sometimes it is just so sweet that the thought of saying goodbye hurts beyond words. This temporal-ness drives me to find truths that are greater, truths that can stand and remain even in the face of great evil and death itself.

The truth of the family of God has helped me as I face the disruption of our biological family. As much as I love my biological family, there is a greater and more enduring family that surpasses my earthly family. And this family is grounded in the eternal family, so to speak, of our Triune God: Father, Son and Holy Spirit. I am continually awed by the reality that we are adopted into this family. Jesus tells us, through is prayer in John 17, that we are loved and made one with the Father even as the Son is one with the Father and eternally beloved. Check this out:

²² *"I have given them the glory you gave me, so **they may be one as we are one.** ²³ **I am in them and you are in me.** May they experience such perfect unity that the world will know that you sent me and **that you love them as much as you love me.** ²⁴ Father, I want these whom you have given me to be with me where I am. Then they can see all the glory you gave me because you loved me even before the world began!"*¹³⁷

This is jaw-dropping truth for all believers. We are made one with one another as we are one with Christ and therefore the Father (and the Holy Spirit¹³⁸.) This is the eternal family to which we belong.

There are lots of other truths that go with this to emphasize and clarify the truth of this ultimate family. We are called the household of God.¹³⁹ We are adopted, in love, by the Father.¹⁴⁰

---

¹³⁷ John 17:22–24

¹³⁸ See 1 Corinthians 12:4–6; 2 Corinthians 13:14; Ephesians 4:4–6; 1 Peter 1:2; Jude 20–21 et al.

¹³⁹ "so that if I am delayed, you will know how people must conduct themselves in the household of God. This is the church of the living God, which is the pillar and foundation of the truth." (1 Timothy 3:15)

¹⁴⁰ "And because we are his children, God has sent the Spirit of his Son into our hearts, prompting us to call out, 'Abba, Father.' " (Galatians 4:6)

"God decided in advance to adopt us into his own family by bringing us to himself through Jesus Christ. This is what he wanted to do, and it gave him great pleasure." (Ephesians 1:5)

"So you have not received a spirit that makes you fearful slaves. Instead, you received God's Spirit when he adopted you as his own children. Now we call him, 'Abba, Father.' " (Romans 8:15)

Jesus is our elder brother. [141] We are joined to countless brothers and sisters in Jesus. [142] We are the bride of Christ himself. [143]

---

[141] "So now Jesus and the ones he makes holy have the same Father. That is why Jesus is not ashamed to call them his brothers and sisters." (Hebrews 2:11)

[142] "Stand firm against him, and be strong in your faith. Remember that your family of believers all over the world is going through the same kind of suffering you are." (1 Peter 5:9)

"Anyone who does God's will is my brother and sister and mother." (Mark 3:35)

"And they sang a new song with these words: "You are worthy to take the scroll and break its seals and open it. For you were slaughtered, and your blood has ransomed people for God from every tribe and language and people and nation." (Revelation 5:9)

"After this I saw a vast crowd, too great to count, from every nation and tribe and people and language, standing in front of the throne and before the Lamb. They were clothed in white robes and held palm branches in their hands." (Revelation 7:9)

[143] "As the Scriptures say, "A man leaves his father and mother and is joined to his wife, and the two are united into one." This is a great mystery, but it is an illustration of the way Christ and the church are one." (Ephesians 5:31–32)

"And I saw the holy city, the new Jerusalem, coming down from God out of heaven like a bride beautifully dressed for her husband. I heard a loud shout from the throne, saying, 'Look, God's home is now among his people! He will live with them, and they will be his people. God himself will be with them. He will wipe every tear from their eyes, and there will be no more death or sorrow or crying or pain. All these things are gone forever.' And the one sitting on the throne said, 'Look, I am making everything

So, the very best my precious biological family can do is to reflect and point to the most precious ultimate family. This ultimately family is the foundation and goal of every biological family. Every family derives its existence from this family.[144] Every family is meant to thrive in the good news of Christ and his kingdom in such a way that they direct all family members towards this ultimate family.[145] So, I must both treasure my biological family and direct all that affection and blessing towards the ultimate goal – to dwell together forever as part of a greater and eternal family. This truth helps me in my sorrow and my joy.

Wednesday, September 28

Yesterday got me thinking about some of the challenges and blessings of raising kids. It is probably the most challenging and significant endeavor we could ever pursue. There are a ton of opinions on how to best raise your family. There are all sorts of

---

new!' And then he said to me, 'Write this down, for what I tell you is trustworthy and true.' " (Revelation 21:2–5)

[144] "For this reason I bow my knees before the Father, from whom every family in heaven and on earth is named," (Ephesians 3:14–15, ESV)

[145] "Children, obey your parents in the Lord, for this is right. "Honor your father and mother" (this is the first commandment with a promise), "that it may go well with you and that you may live long in the land." Fathers, do not provoke your children to anger, but bring them up in the discipline and instruction of the Lord." (Ephesians 6:1–4, ESV)

"Did he not make them one, with a portion of the Spirit in their union? And what was the one God seeking? Godly offspring. So guard yourselves in your spirit, and let none of you be faithless to the wife of your youth." (Malachi 2:15, ESV)

implicit and explicit pressures on family life. There are so many unspoken expectations. It takes a lot of wisdom, hard work and grit to do what is right and best. And no wisdom or hard work can succeed apart from faith, humility, honesty and lots of prayer. And, no parent is meant to go it alone – grandparents, pastors, friends and peers are all needed for counsel and practical support. And most of all, it is imperative to let God speak and lead by his word in the power of the Spirit. The wisdom from the mainstream culture can be helpful at times and harmful at other times. We can learn much from experts. But we must ultimately rely on the things God has clearly given us in his word. His word is sufficient to give us the core things we need for all of life, including parenting.

We have found the simple instructions in Ephesians 6:1-4 to be profoundly helpful. It says,

> *"Fathers, do not provoke your children to anger by the way you treat them. Rather, bring them up with the discipline and instruction that comes from the Lord."*[146]

This verse calls dads (moms are involved here too!) to not treat their kids in a way that frustrates their kids. They are not to dominate or discourage their kids. As often in the Bible, a negative command implies a positive command. So, the positive side of this is that parents should do all they can to inspire and encourage their kids – to speak to them and lead them so that they find the strength and perspective to do good.

---

[146] Ephesians 6:1–4,

We have seen this work so effectively in our children's lives. It seems that our encouragement and affirmation was like pixie dust. Every time we took time to encourage our kids about explicit characteristics or actions we saw, it had a magical effect on their disposition. It wasn't always immediate, sometimes it took a while. But it so often worked wonders in them. We would see them be more eager to do good, more willing to believe and trust God, kinder to their siblings, less mopey and more cheerful. Conversely, when we weren't careful with our words it was like poison that sapped their vitality and joy. And sadly, we have seen many other kids who seemed drained and exasperated by parents who had too many discouraging things to say and not enough encouraging things. We understand how easy it is to go that way. But we had to work hard to correct ourselves and aim more of 90% encouragement, 10% correction. Thankfully, I think we did alright and enjoyed the good fruit that comes from following through on Ephesians 6:4.

This verse tells us to bring up our children in the discipline and instruction that comes from the Lord. This means that both the content of our teaching and the lifestyle we are calling them to follow are from the Lord. First, this means it must center on the truth of the good news of Jesus Christ, the grace and mercy we have in him for our sins and full redemption. Our kids need to hear and see what a life centered on the glorious good news of grace looks like. Second, this means our teaching and modeling must be with God at the center – God in all of his glory, all of the truth of the Trinity, all of the wonder of his revelation through creation and his word. The goodness and glory of God must saturate all our parenting. Third, this means our instruction and lifestyle must be in line with his good and perfect law. All that makes for the deepest love for God and the most thorough love for our fellow man should guide us in what we are doing as parents.

Such glorious and lofty goals should inspire us but also drive us to see our needs. We as parents need these truths. We need mercy and grace. We need Jesus. We need the Father's love and generosity. We need the Spirit's power. We need to show our kids that we are learning to love these things but will never measure up this side of heaven. Therefore, like them, we need the bloody cross and the empty grave, every moment, every day. They should see us quick to confess our sins and cry out for forgiveness and help. They should know our weaknesses and desperate need even as we know theirs. Hope you can see the impact of this one powerful verse on parenting. There are many others, but I think Ephesians 6:4 is a great starting point.

Thursday, September 29

Parenting doesn't stop once the kids reach adulthood. It just shifts to being more like a mentor and older friend. In some ways, the challenges of parenting adult children can be harder than parenting young children. Once they are adults you no longer have the sort of leverage to control their decisions and their outcomes. You have to release them to make their own decisions and the mistakes that come with it. Hopefully, you've had a lot of practice as throughout their teen years. The M.O. should shift once they are no longer younger children. But it transitions over the ten or so years from young childhood to adulthood. They shouldn't find the transition to making adult decisions an abrupt change at 18. Nevertheless, the point of adulthood is the end of parental prerogative over decisions and outcomes. That can be a real temptation for any parent. We all know just how important the key decisions of young adulthood can be and we also know how little we knew at that age. Many a parent of young adults have spent sleepless nights in prayer for their children. Perhaps this phase is more about the parents' growth than the child's. We must learn to let go and trust God and love and advise our children without trying to control them.

My son, Matthias, has given me permission to share an illustration from his life. Matthias is a passionate and self-motivated man. He also loves God. When he turned 18, he was deeply affected by the things we were learning about North Korea. As much of the world was transitioning to a new age of political peace and flourishing, North Korea was finally being exposed for all the horror and murder that had gone on. Then North Korea launched nuclear missiles on Beijing, Seoul and Tokyo. Thankfully they were unsuccessful because of anti-missile satellites. The Coalition of Nations acted to invade North Korea and Matthias signed up for the North American Marine Forces.

Now, we have tremendous respect for the role and heroism of our armed forces, but Matthias knew little of what he was getting into and hadn't consulted us when he signed up. Had he asked, we would likely have given our blessing but perhaps suggested some alternative ways to serve that would better suit his gifts and his ability to help the cause such as ROTC or the Air Forces. As it was, he got a crash course in the brutalities of war and evil. Thankfully, he survived, and the Coalition of Nations forces prevailed within 18 months. And thankfully, Matthias came back more mature and more committed to Jesus. But he had to battle lingering trauma from all that he saw. And his mother and I and all his loved ones had to endure many nights full of tears and prayers as we heard the latest from the front.

All-in-all, we saw God use this very difficult time to teach us more about his faithfulness and our desperate need for him. We learned about how ridiculous it is to think we can control much of anything. We learned the real power of persistent and regular prayer. We learned the depths of our love for our children are a drop in the bucket compared to the vast love of God for his own Son and therefore all his children. And Matthias learned to trust God in similar ways. He also learned that he needs the counsel and benefit of older brothers and sisters as he seeks to navigate through life. I can say that now Matthias is one of my very best friends and I his, as well.

I hope that helps illustrate the key aspects of parenting adult children. God is never finished with us as parents and as children. And although many aspects of the roles may change, we still remain connected by the bonds of family and desperately needy of God's sustaining grace and presence in our lives.

Friday, September 30

A little more on family stuff today. First, just want to talk a little bit about the joys of being a grandparent. Abby and I loved being parents and so often, when we see young parents or watch our grandchildren at play, are almost brought to tears as we remember so many happy years with little ones. But we have found being grandparents to be a special blessing. It seems that it contains so much of the wonder and joy of having children with so little of the responsibilities and hard work of being their parents. Our oldest grandchild, Marie, is 16. Our youngest so far, Saphia, is 2. We have 11 total: Marie 16, Aafreen 14, John 13, Luke 12, Zana 12, Evelyn 10, Soroush 9, Farzad 7, Patrick 7, Ervin 5 and Saphia 2. The ones with Persian names belong to Zoey and Arman, the others belong to Matthias and Isabella. Our two youngest children, Sophia and Liam, aren't married and appear very happy as singles. Their lives are very full, and they are a great aunt and uncle.

Anyhow, we love being grandparents. And we love sharing our grandchildren with others in the church, especially the older singles who never had kids. They are all called "Auntie" or "Uncle", both by our kids when they were young and now by our grandchildren. Although our parish is about 1,000 people, it does feel like one big family. And our grandchildren are very rich in grandparents and great aunts and uncles. And it gives us so much joy to watch how our single friends light up when they have opportunities to watch the kids or just interact with them. I think God intended us to live in such community – a multigenerational, multiethnic family full of the life and mission of God. We are always seeing new people added and have had the privilege of sending many to other churches and mission opportunities. We also have had to say goodbye to so many dear beloved friends who have finished their course in this life. But we are so thankful for the hope we have, a sure and certain hope, of eternal resurrection life, where grandparents are present. Thankfully, we will be there with new bodies and unending youthfulness after the same pattern of the resurrected Christ.

One other thing I wanted to mention on parenting that has application to all of life: parenting and life are an interplay between grace and law. Both must be present in proper measure and interconnected. Grace is anything that is an undeserved blessing. There are little things that are grace, and huge things. Beautiful days, sunshine, rainbows, food, clothing, shelter are all grace. As well as full and final atonement, acceptance and adoption by God, the new birth and presence of the Holy Spirit, the Church, eternal life and union with the Trinity, these are all grace. We only truly live by grace.

But grace is also connected to law. Law is the moral will of God. It is the command to do right and not do wrong. It is summed up as loving God and loving our neighbor. But it includes the details of love. Law never earns grace, but grace empowers law keeping. And if we truly grasp and receive grace. we will be free and joyful law keepers.

All this relates to parenting because we want to be instruments of grace and law in our children's lives. We want to so bring these two aspects of relating to God that our children learn how to walk with God and live in his universe themselves. We must learn to live this way in the regular rhythms of our days and weeks and seasons. And we must instruct our children and those under our charge in the same. So much of my job as a pastor has been to lead God's people in the interplay between grace and law.

This is part of why I have included liturgies or prayers at the end of each week of journaling. The liturgies of our lives, whatever they may be, will establish us in related lifestyles. If we have liturgies of worship that reinforce grace and law we will find ourselves practicing fulfilling and effective lifestyles. We will live in the goodness of God, for his glory and for the great blessing of those around us. As you read through these various prayers at the end of each week, I hope you can parse out the dynamic flow of grace and law in the life of the follower of Christ.

Saturday, October 1

O boy, I got an update on my sentence yesterday. Even though I am in a jail cell much of each day, I sometimes forget that my sentence, likely death by execution, is imminent. I had to sign a document attesting that I am disregarding the court's offer to release me. This offer depends on my commitment to no longer speak publicly about anything on their long list of what they consider misanthropic. That list includes things like the supremacy of Christ, the reality of sin, the necessity of faith and repentance, the law of God as supreme and multiple things that could be construed as unfavorable portrayal of "The Messengers" and their allies. So, after a long pause and some heavy sighs, I signed it. When I lifted the pen from the touchscreen, I realized I had just signed my death sentence.

They also gave me more details on the "final solution" itself. They offer a range of options, including forced rehabilitation through medical means on one end and termination of life on the other. Termination of life options include death by injections. First you receive benzodiazepine for anti-anxiety before receiving sodium thiopental to induce unconsciousness, pancuronium bromide to stop your breathing and then potassium chloride to stop your heart. The other choice for execution options is death by starvation. This is an option for the inmate who refuses the lethal injection option. They are given the choice to

141

starve themselves to death. Either way, it will be a brutal end and the thought of it is making me feel like another panic attack is coming.

O Lord, give me strength in all of this. Give me strength to think through what to do. Give me strength to live each day one day at a time, trusting you for the grace of that day. Help me remember that the final day will hold all the grace I need from you to get through it. And strengthen me with the joy of knowing my risen Savior will be there at the finish line cheering me on and waiting for me in front of that vast crowd of witnesses cheering on all who cross the finish line![147]

Sunday, October 2

Sorry to diverge from the theme for this week, parenting and family life. When I received the update on my execution it was all I could think about. But I want to finish this week with a liturgy on the family. I hope this blesses your Sunday worship!

---

[147] "Therefore, since we are surrounded by such a huge crowd of witnesses to the life of faith, let us strip off every weight that slows us down, especially the sin that so easily trips us up. And let us run with endurance the race God has set before us. We do this by keeping our eyes on Jesus, the champion who initiates and perfects our faith. Because of the joy awaiting him, he endured the cross, disregarding its shame. Now he is seated in the place of honor beside God's throne." (Hebrews 12:1–2).

Family Worship for Matins/Sext/Vespers[148]

Opening/Greeting: (*Choose* one of the following, or another text appropriate to the church calendar)

Ordinary Time: "May God our Father and the Lord Jesus Christ give you grace and peace." (Philippians 1:2)

Epiphany: "But my name is honored by people of other nations from morning till night. All around the world they offer sweet incense and pure offerings in honor of my name. For my name is great among the nations," says the LORD of Heaven's Armies." (Malachi 1:11)

Lent: "If we claim we have no sin, we are only fooling ourselves and not living in the truth. But if we confess our sins to him, he is faithful and just to forgive us our sins and to cleanse us from all wickedness." (1 John 1:8–9)

Holy Week: "All of us, like sheep, have strayed away. We have left God's paths to follow our own. Yet the LORD laid on him the sins of us all." (Isaiah 53:6)

---

[148] Adapted from Family Worship, Brian Moats, Theopolic Institute, https://theopolisinstitute.com/a-family-liturgy/

Easter Season, Ascension Day, Pentecost, Ordinary Time:

Alleluia! Christ is Risen.

The Lord is risen indeed. Alleluia!

"This is the day the LORD has made. We will rejoice and be glad in it." (Psalm 118:24)

"But thank God! He gives us victory over sin and death through our Lord Jesus Christ." (1 Corinthians 15:57)

Confession of Sin   *Psalm* 51:10-12 can be sung or recited as an introduction.

Dad: Dear family, we have come together in the presence of Almighty God our heavenly Father, to give thanks for the great benefits that we have received at His hands, to set forth His most worthy praise, to hear His holy Word, and to ask, for ourselves and on behalf of others, those things that are necessary for life and salvation. And so that we may prepare ourselves in heart and mind to worship him, let us with penitent and obedient hearts confess our sins, that we may obtain forgiveness by His infinite goodness and mercy.

(And/or)   Let us humbly confess our sins to Almighty God.

Silent confession:

Together:	Almighty and most merciful Father, We have erred and strayed from your ways like lost sheep, We have followed too much the devices and desires of our own hearts, We have offended against your holy laws, We have left undone those things which we ought to have done, And we have done those things which we ought not to have done, and there is no health in us, But you, O Lord, have mercy upon us, Spare us who confess our faults, Restore those who are penitent, According to your promises declared unto mankind in Christ Jesus our Lord; And grant, O most merciful Father, for His sake, That we may hereafter live a godly, righteous, and sober life, To the glory of Your holy Name. Amen.
Dad:	The Almighty and merciful Lord grants us absolution and remission of all our sins, repentance, amendment of life, and the grace of his Holy Spirit. Amen
Dad:	O Lord, open our lips.
Family:	And our mouth shall show forth thy praise.

145

Family (sung):	Glory be to the Father, and to the Son, and to the Holy Ghost: as it was in the beginning, is now, and ever shall be, world without end. Amen. Or (sung) Praise God from whom all blessing flow, praise Him all creatures here below, Praise Him above ye heavenly hosts, Praise Father, Son, and Holy Ghost. Amen
The Psalm:	The Psalm of the Day from the Book of Common Worship.
The Lesson(s):	A reading from the passage of the Day from the Book of Common Worship. After each Lesson the Reader may say: The Word of the Lord. Answer: Thanks be to God. Open discussion and teaching from the Bible reading.
Prayer Time:	Share requests and petitions to one another. Then we all pray for specific items.

	Dad concludes the prayers and leads the family into the Lord's prayer.
Dad:	Let us pray:
Family:	The Lord's Prayer Our Father who is in heaven, may your Name be hallowed May your Kingdom come. May your will be done on earth, as it is in heaven. Give us today the food we need, and forgive us our sins, as we forgive those who sin against us. And don't let us yield to temptation, but rescue us from the evil one.

Singing of Hymns and Psalms

Chosen that evening by dad or the family.
"Sing praises to God, sing praises; sing praises to our King, sing praises!"
(Psalm 47:6)

A Collect of the Day from the Book of Common Worship

Conclusion:

Dad:	The grace of our Lord Jesus Christ, and the love of God, and the fellowship of the Holy Spirit, be with us all.
All:	*Amen!*

Following Worship: One or two age-appropriate recitations from The Book of Common Worship: Children's Catechism

Chapter 9: Something Beautiful

Monday, October 3

This week, I want to journal about beauty and the arts. I know I've talked about it already in various ways, but the topic is worthy of special attention. Beauty has been an important part of creation and the human experience since the very beginning. When God made everything, he pronounced it "good." This goodness was a thorough goodness, full of truth and beauty, function and blessing. When he made humankind, male and female, he pronounced them as "very good."

Later, the woman was tempted by the serpent in

the beauty of the forbidden fruit. *"The woman was convinced. She saw that the tree was beautiful, and its fruit looked delicious, and she wanted the wisdom it would give her. So she took some of the fruit and ate it. Then she gave some to her husband, who was with her, and he ate it, too."*[149]

Beauty, attached to a corrupted truth and perverse goodness, was powerful enough to lure Eve and Adam into rejecting what is most true, good, and beautiful – God himself and life in his kingdom.

Moving to the other end of the Bible, we see the New Jerusalem as truly stunning, a beautiful bride for Christ. Revelation 22 presents this picture.

---

[149] Genesis 3:6

"Then I saw a new heaven and a new earth, for the old heaven and the old earth had disappeared. And the sea was also gone. ² And I saw the holy city, the new Jerusalem, coming down from God out of heaven like a bride beautifully dressed for her husband…⁹ Then one of the seven angels who held the seven bowls containing the seven last plagues came and said to me, 'Come with me! I will show you the bride, the wife of the Lamb.' ¹⁰ So he took me in the Spirit to a great, high mountain, and he showed me the holy city, Jerusalem, descending out of heaven from God. ¹¹ It shone with the glory of God and sparkled like a precious stone-like jasper as clear as crystal. ¹² The city wall was broad and high, with twelve gates guarded by twelve angels. And the names of the twelve tribes of Israel were written on the gates. ¹³ There were three gates on each side – east, north, south, and west. ¹⁴ The wall of the city had twelve foundation stones, and on them were written the names of the twelve apostles of the Lamb.

¹⁵ The angel who talked to me held in his hand a gold measuring stick to measure the city, its gates, and its wall. ¹⁶ When he measured it, he found it was a square, as wide as it was long. In fact, its length and width, and height were each 1,400 miles. ¹⁷ Then, he measured the walls and found them to be 216 feet thick (according to the human standard used by the angel).

¹⁸ The wall was made of jasper, and the city was pure gold, as clear as glass. ¹⁹ The wall of the city was built on foundation stones inlaid with twelve precious stones: the first was jasper, the second sapphire, the third agate, the fourth emerald, ²⁰ the fifth onyx, the sixth carnelian, the seventh chrysolite, the eighth beryl,

the ninth topaz, the tenth chrysoprase, the eleventh jacinth, the twelfth amethyst.

²¹ The twelve gates were made of pearls – each gate from a single pearl! And the main street was pure gold, as clear as glass.

²² I saw no temple in the city, for the Lord God Almighty and the Lamb are its temple. ²³ And the city has no need of sun or moon, for the glory of God illuminates the city, and the Lamb is its light. ²⁴ The nations will walk in its light, and the kings of the world will enter the city in all their glory."[150]

So, all that to say beauty matters. What is pleasing to see or hear, experience or contemplate, is beauty. And beauty is best when fully in harmony with what is good and true. The more thorough the goodness, truth, and beauty of something, the more glorious it is. Such beauty needn't be a shallow simplistic physical beauty. The scars our Savior bears are most beautiful. Similarly, the stripes on the back of St. Paul and many other martyrs will be part of the glory of their resurrected bodies. Beauty includes the physical but can include various dimensions beyond simple proportionality and purity of form. I firmly believe such beauty is dear to the heart of God.

Tuesday, October 4

I'm sitting here in my stark cell, a simple bed, a small desk, a plastic chair, and a bookshelf, a video monitor, a metal sink, and a toilet, surrounded by cinder block walls painted pale mint green. Under my feet is a cold concrete floor painted gray. Over

---

[150] Revelation 21

my head is a white ceiling with sealed lights controlled by some-one else. I can look out of my cell through a barred window in a metal door to see a hallway lit with fluorescent lights. Although it provides a safe and relatively comfortable place for me, it certainly wouldn't be considered beautiful by anybody. It is functional. But it supplies little inspiration and kinda acts like a sedative to any creative impulses.

But, I have known so much beauty in my life. And although I sit here in the starkness of my cell, I can recall so many vivid scenes full of such intense beauty. I am reminded of the poem *"I Wandered Lonely as a Cloud"* by William Wordsworth.

I wandered lonely as a cloud
That floats on high o'er vales and hills,
When all at once I saw a crowd,
A host of golden daffodils;
Beside the lake, beneath the trees,
Fluttering and dancing in the breeze.

Continuous as the stars that shine
And twinkle on the milky way,
They stretched in never-ending line
Along the margin of a bay:
Ten thousand saw I at a glance,
Tossing their heads in sprightly dance.

The waves beside them danced; but they
Out-did the sparkling waves in glee:
A poet could not but be gay,

In such a jocund company:
I gazed – and gazed – but little thought
What wealth the show to me had brought:

For oft, when on my couch I lie
In vacant or in pensive mood,
They flash upon that inward eye
Which is the bliss of solitude;
And then my heart with pleasure fills,
And dances with the daffodils.

Whether it is a memory of daffodils or cherub-like children shrieking with glee as I dip with them in the ocean waves, my memories of beautiful moments transport me from this stark cell to somewhere full of beauty and goodness.

And my life has thousands of such memories. And should I live to be twice my age, I could fill my mind with many more and yet new memories of that which is beautiful.

Surely, this establishes something very fundamental about God. Romans 1:20 tells us, *"For his invisible attributes, namely, his eternal power and divine nature, have been clearly perceived, ever since the creation of the world, in the things that have been made."*[151] God is beautiful and the author of all beauty. He obviously treasures beauty. And we know him better through seeing and

---

[151] Romans 1:20a, (ESV)

experiencing beauty. And when we see him face-to-face, we will be overwhelmed with his infinite beauty.

Wednesday, October 5

I wanted to reflect on beauty in the form of art, images, and craftmanship. I am so grateful for the many gifted people who express the beauty of creation through various works like paintings, sculptures, architecture, landscaping, and visually-appealing technological items. As we gaze at God's creation, we see so much that is visually stunning and beautiful on many levels. It is a terrible tragedy to miss how important beauty is to God, as seen so clearly in creation. If someone remains unconvinced of God's commitment to art and visual beauty, there is much in scripture to convince us he cares about art. Looking, as we already have, at the bookends of the Bible, we read in Genesis 1 *"God looked over all he had made, and he saw that it was very good!"*[152] We go to the end of the Bible, and we see the stunning visual beauty portrayed in Revelation 21.

> *"The twelve gates were made of pearls – each gate from a single pearl! And the main street was pure gold, as clear as glass. I saw no temple in the city, for the Lord God Almighty and the Lamb are its temple. And the city has no need of sun or moon, for the glory of God illuminates the city, and the Lamb is its light."*
> Revelation 21:21–23,

In the book of Exodus God instructs the craftsman Bezalel to devise artistic designs in the creation of the tabernacle, the

---

[152] Genesis 1:31

154

place of worship for the Israelites at the time.[153] He commissions images of Cherubim to be woven into the fabric of the tabernacle[154] and set on the Ark of the Covenant[155].

The prohibition of forming images does not apply to legitimate representation of things in creation but images that would be objects of worship themselves. It is not the proper enjoyment and exercise of our God-given artistic talents that is wrong. It is using these talents to create something that would become the focus rather than the facilitator of our worship of the true God. The true God cannot be contained in any created item. Thus, Paul in Romans specifies it is exchanging the glory of God, the infinitely glorious Creator, for the subservient glory of created things.[156] But the true God is experienced through

---

[153] "Then Moses told the people of Israel, "The LORD has specifically chosen Bezalel son of Uri, grandson of Hur, of the tribe of Judah. The LORD has filled Bezalel with the Spirit of God, giving him great wisdom, ability, and expertise in all kinds of crafts. He is a master craftsman, expert in working with gold, silver, and bronze. He is skilled in engraving and mounting gemstones and in carving wood. He is a master at every craft." (Exodus 35:30–33)

[154] "Make the Tabernacle from ten curtains of finely woven linen. Decorate the curtains with blue, purple, and scarlet thread and with skillfully embroidered cherubim." (Exodus 26:1)

[155] "Then make two cherubim from hammered gold, and place them on the two ends of the atonement cover." (Exodus 25:18)

[156] "Yes, they knew God, but they wouldn't worship him as God or even give him thanks. And they began to think up foolish ideas of what God was like. As a result, their minds became dark and confused. Claiming to be wise, they instead became utter fools. And instead of worshiping the glorious,

his created order as it serves as the means of facilitating the experience of his glory because it is the expression of his glory while not containing or limiting the vastness of his glory and his being.[157] Furthermore, the creation is not God but an expression of God's glory.[158]

Given all this, we should understand that art and craftmanship are expressions of the very image of God in us and should be pursued with enthusiasm and excellence for the purpose of

---

ever-living God, they worshiped idols made to look like mere people and birds and animals and reptiles. So God abandoned them to do whatever shameful things their hearts desired. As a result, they did vile and degrading things with each other's bodies. They traded the truth about God for a lie. So they worshiped and served the things God created instead of the Creator himself, who is worthy of eternal praise! Amen." (Romans 1:21–25)

[157] CF: "I can never escape from your Spirit! I can never get away from your presence! If I go up to heaven, you are there; if I go down to the grave, you are there. If I ride the wings of the morning, if I dwell by the farthest oceans, even there your hand will guide me, and your strength will support me." (Psalm 139:7–10) and "Am I a God who is only close at hand?" says the LORD. "No, I am far away at the same time. Can anyone hide from me in a secret place? Am I not everywhere in all the heavens and earth?" says the LORD." (Jeremiah 23:23–24)

[158] CF: "You are worthy, O Lord our God, to receive glory and honor and power. For you created all things, and they exist because you created what you pleased." (Revelation 4:11), "O LORD, our Lord, your majestic name fills the earth! Your glory is higher than the heavens. You have taught children and infants to tell of your strength, silencing your enemies and all who oppose you. When I look at the night sky and see the work of your fingers – the moon and the stars you set in place" (Psalm 8:1–3) and "The heavens proclaim the glory of God. The skies display his craftsmanship." (Psalm 19:1).

glorifying God and helping those made in his image better enjoy real experiences of his unfathomable goodness and glory.

Thursday, October 6

Today, I want to venture into the art of paintings and sculpture. I am no expert here, but I have some thoughts that I hope will help show the place of art in a Christian view of the world. I love the painting by Renoir entitled "Two-Sisters (On the Terrace)." It is a simple scene, an older and younger sister dressed up and perhaps getting ready to get a knitting lesson from a favorite relative. The colors on the sisters are vibrant and focus your eye on their feminine beauty. The scenery behind them is more monochromatic, highlighting the beauty of the two girls set against a serene and simple backdrop. You can't help but appreciate God's genius in creating mankind and setting this image of his glory as the crown of his creation.

Another favorite of mine is "The Starry Night." When you look at this painting, you feel what it is like to stare at the sky on a beautiful clear night. No photo can capture the feelings conveyed in this masterpiece. The glowing stars, the effervescent moon, the swirling clouds framed by the village, and the rolling hills convey the glory of the heavens, while the village church's steeple directs us to behold something greater than our mere surroundings. The dark cypress tree seems to threaten to overshadow the glory of the heavens with the darkness of a lost soul. All this exists in one masterful painting. God's creativity is on grand display through the work of Vincent Van Gogh, a man made in God's image.

I really enjoy almost everything done by Michelangelo Buonarroti. He had a tremendous gift for sculpture, painting, poetry, and architecture. Although some interpret his poems on platonic love as homoerotic, there is nothing to indicate they were more than a healthy brotherly love. Deep brotherly or sisterly love is too often twisted by cultures that have no place for non-sexual same-sex relationships. His writings show he was a man of Christian faith and deep love for others. He wrote near the end of his life, *"Neither painting nor sculpture will be able any longer to calm my soul, now turned toward that divine love that opened his arms on the cross to take us in."*[159]

Michelangelo's "Creation of Adam" pictures the moment God imparted spiritual life to Adam, that he might bear his image, body, and soul. Adam's form is beautiful but barely alive as it awaits the divine touch of his Heavenly Father. God is depicted human-like yet clothed in white, bending towards Adam and reaching out with his right hand as Adam awaits his divine touch. Under the left arm of the Father is a young woman. The Father reaches out over the woman and touches a boy. It is likely that Michelangelo meant this boy to be Jesus. It was as if the Father was creating the first Adam while anticipating the Second Adam. This Second Adam is to come through the woman under God's left arm. She is Eve and/or Mary, the mother of the living. This amazing painting is an excellent example of the beauty and depth of truth and goodness captured in art. None of the nudity in this depiction connotes an abusive view of the body – either in degrading the body for sexual immorality or shaming the

---

[159] Michelangelo Poem 285, The Poetry of Michelangelo, translated by James M. Saslow, Copyright ©1991 Yale University Press.

body, as often happens from the influence of Gnostic here-
sies.[160]

Similarly, Michelangelo's sculptures depict the union of the
human body and soul through the skillful presentation of his
subjects. His famous "David" presents this biblical hero confi-
dent but tense for battle against the blasphemer, Goliath,
wearing no armor, equipped simply with his sling. David's no-
bility and determination are clearly seen in this marvelous
sculpture.

Michelangelo's "Pieta" depicts the Virgin Mary holding the
body of her crucified son. The expressions on both their faces
are striking. Jesus' face is serene, conveying peace even in his
death, pointing to his victory over sin and death through his
crucifixion. Mary is sad but serene, mourning the death of her
son but with faith and peace. The sculpture is remarkable in all
the emotion and truth it conveys in marble.

All these works and those like them are wonderful examples
of the place of beauty and the arts in conveying the true and the

---

[160] Much of the abuse of the human body derives from Gnostic heresy.
Gnosticism divides the spiritual from the physical, elevating the spiritual
and degrading the physical. This degradation would be either in shaming
the human body or degrading the human body in sexual immorality. It has
been a long-standing heresy that has influenced the Church too much. A
biblical view understands that body and soul are both very good as made by
God and made to flourish together according to God's good order, with
proper regard and treatment of each as a functioning union. To be human
is to be both body and soul in proper relationship to God and one another.
This is true holiness.

good. We are better off for them and should celebrate the God-given gift of art. Such art is a clear sign that we are made in the image of God to re-create after our glorious Creator.

Friday, October 7th

Unlike items like paintings and sculptures, architecture and technology often carry with them a strong pragmatic component. A home has to house people. A car must transport people. But who wants to live in a concrete box for a house? Who wants to drive a metal tube with wheels? The use of art is a key part to the full enjoyment of architecture and technology. Buildings and technological items must function well but ought to be beautiful in some complementary way.

The best-loved architecture uses style and art to visually enjoy the building. The strip malls so common in North America may be convenient, but they are not beautiful. Massive housing complexes built by various governments in the 20th century may provide a place to live, but their bleak architecture seems to have contributed to the bleak outlook often held by those who dwelled there.

But Victorian-style buildings, housing storefronts built into a community of apartments and offices, lining a landscaped boulevard will be a place residents and shoppers would be glad to live and spend time shopping and just enjoying the surroundings. The early part of the 21st century saw the reintroduction of planned housing built on this design. One example, among many, is Frisco, Texas, NAU. The Frisco Square area was planned and developed in the early 21st century as Frisco grew faster than most other cities in the NAU. Instead of merely building functional residential and commercial buildings, disconnected from one another, Frisco planned and built a new downtown that reproduced the many features of architecture and urban living that best serve the true, good and beautiful. To walk around Frisco Square feels like walking around an older European city, with beautiful buildings, street-level shopping, townhomes, repurposed factory buildings, and a beautiful church on the town green. It is the sort of community that not only functions well but reflects the deeper values of community, beauty, and rest.

Technology also is better served by incorporating beauty. A compact box-like car might be efficient and economical at getting you from point A to point B. But you would probably rather rent a Rolls Royce for a wedding. If you were able, you would park your box-like car and rent a convertible sports car for that special vacation drive along the coast. And who can help but admire the artistry in motion of a 2021 Aston Martin Valkyrie, a 1963 Corvette Stingray, or a 2053 Mercedes Benz GT Roadster as they drive along the highway?

This principle of beauty and function can be seen behind many successful technological advances. Apple Computer changed the computing world with the focus on aesthetics in personal computing. Appliance companies must make products that are functional but also look good in your kitchen. Video monitors that double as displays for portraits or master-pieces of art are more appealing than an obtrusive monitor that invades a living space. A neat and well-ordered workshop with tools properly stored and displayed is much more inviting than a hodge-podge of tools and trash strewn about a workbench.

Beauty in technology and architecture is important. We are created in the image of God, and therefore beauty always matters even when we are doing things as pragmatic as housing or transporting ourselves. I am grateful for all the beautiful ways we can experience life in God's good creation!

Saturday, October 8th

I don't get to listen to much music in prison. Some of the prisoners get to listen to music, but those here for political crimes like mine are shut off from music. But that doesn't keep me from listening to songs in my mind and humming or singing along. I especially like remembering my very talented wife's voice and the songs she wrote and played on one of the ten different instruments she played. She was amazing. She learned guitar, piano, violin, and banjo as a kid. She took up the flute and the French Horn later. She figured out how to play the harp on her own. She is a gifted drummer and percussionist. And she even has played the tuba. Anyhow, as you can guess, music has been a big part of our family. I have liked all types of music since I was a kid, but Abby introduced me to greater depths of pretty much every type of music.

I really miss listening to jazz as I read, classical and epic soundtracks as I study, rock as I work out, swing music while dancing or having a party, rap while driving, country on long road trips, piano while praying, and all types of gospel and worship music when doing everything else. The silence here in prison has been an opportunity to concentrate on prayer and thinking a little more, but I miss having my surroundings filled with music.

Music is a wonderful gift from God. God himself is portrayed as singing in the Bible.[161] There are over 300 references to music in the Bible, the great majority are positive. Music was an integral part of the worship in the Temple.[162] David was hired to sing and drive away spiritual darkness from King Saul.[163] There will be singing in heaven beyond anything we have ever heard.[164]

---

[161] "For the LORD your God is living among you. He is a mighty savior. He will take delight in you with gladness. With his love, he will calm all your fears. He will rejoice over you with joyful songs." (Zephaniah 3:17)

[162] "Shimea, Haggiah, and Asaiah. David assigned the following men to lead the music at the house of the LORD after the Ark was placed there. They ministered with music at the Tabernacle until Solomon built the Temple of the LORD in Jerusalem. They carried out their work, following all the regulations handed down to them." (1 Chronicles 6:30–32)

[163] "And whenever the tormenting spirit from God troubled Saul, David would play the harp. Then Saul would feel better, and the tormenting spirit would go away." (1 Samuel 16:23)

[164] "And when he took the scroll, the four living beings and the twenty-four elders fell down before the Lamb. Each one had a harp, and they held gold bowls filled with incense, which are the prayers of God's people. And they sang a new song with these words: "You are worthy to take the scroll and break its seals and open it. For you were slaughtered, and your blood has ransomed people for God from every tribe and language and people and nation. And you have caused them to become a Kingdom of priests for our God. And they will reign on the earth." Then I looked again, and I heard the voices of thousands and millions of angels around the throne and of the living beings and the elders. And they sang in a mighty chorus: "Worthy is the Lamb who was slaughtered – to receive power and riches and wisdom and strength and honor and glory and blessing." And then I heard every

Music seems to have a powerful effect in both expressing the depths of our souls but also speaking to and directing those depths. It is a powerful medium that can be used powerfully for good or powerfully for evil, like so many other amazing things in God's creation. Even though I can't listen to music while here, I still hear so many of these songs and works in my mind's ear. And the words of so many great hymns and songs echo in my ears and help my heart find a resting place amidst my struggles and my wanderings.

Sunday, October 9 – Today, I leave you with two prayers for artists. Enjoy!

A Prayer for Artists[165]

Lord, remember your artists. Have mercy upon them and remember with compassion all those that reflect the good, the ill, the strengths, and the weaknesses of the human spirit.

Remember those who raise their voices in unending song, those who pour their souls into music loud and soft.

---

creature in heaven and on earth and under the earth and in the sea. They sang: "Blessing and honor and glory and power belong to the one sitting on the throne and to the Lamb forever and ever." And the four living beings said, "Amen!" And the twenty-four elders fell down and worshiped the Lamb." (Revelation 5:8–14)

[165] From Bryan Brown, worship pastor at Christ Church in Austin and the worship leader of the Transforming Culture symposium in 2008, adapted from Herbert Whittaker's "Prayer for the Artists" (1987).

Remember those who put pigment to surface, carve wood and stone and marble, who work base metals into beauty, those building upwards from the earth toward heaven.

Remember those who put thought to paper by computer and by the pen; the poets who delve, the playwrights who analyze and proclaim, the dreamers-up of narrative, all those who work with the light and shadows of film.

Remember the actors moved by Spirit and dancers moving through space.

Remember all these artists whom you have placed among us, for are they not, O Lord, the fellows of your inspiration? Do they not, Lord God, bring to your people great proof of your divinity and our part in it?

Remember your artists and show them mercy and compassion that they may do the same and so uplift all your people. That they may cry forth your praises, as we do here.

Amen! Amen! Amen!

A Prayer for Church Musicians and Artists[166]

O God, whom saints and angels delight to worship in heaven: Be ever-present with your servants on earth who seek through art and music to perfect the praises of your people. Grant them even now true

---

[166] Book of Common Prayer, 2019, Anglican Church in America, Prayers and Thanksgiving, Item 14 Prayer for Sound Government. See bcp2019.anglicanchurch.net

glimpses of your beauty, and make them worthy at length to behold it unveiled for evermore; through Jesus Christ our Lord. Amen.

Chapter 10: Killing Me Softly

Monday, October 10

I have a big decision to make by the end of this week. What way will I choose for my final sentence? Regardless, it will mean the end of my life as I have known it. The milder methods, if you can call them that, involve some form of alteration of who I am through medical means.

A common method that has emerged in the past ten years or so is the use of a brain implant to control impulses and supply dopamine incentives for preferred behavior and headaches and dysphoria for bad behavior. It has worked very effectively. In my case, if I choose this, anytime I say the wrong thing or am in the wrong place, I will receive a punishment. Every time I say or do anything that supports what they consider healthy behavior, I will get a reward. The end result is control of the individual as desired.

Another method they offered is to install a permanent port to feed me with a steady stream of sedatives and mood-altering drugs to basically eliminate any creative thought or self-assertion. This is basically a chemical lobotomy. They also provide a "new and improved" surgical lobotomy that permanently eliminates personal motivation, intellectual depth, and most emotion.

Next on the list is death by lethal injection, as I described a couple of weeks ago. And then, there is death by starvation – where they isolate you and let you starve to death, providing only water but no nutrients.

I never thought I would have to think through my choice of death in light of God's truth. I always figured it would be chosen for me – maybe heart failure, maybe an accident, maybe even violent martyrdom. But I never thought I would do the choosing. How does one choose such a thing?

First, I am not opting for the death of self via a brain implant or drugs, or surgery. This is the death of self plus an opportunity for the government to parade around an example to dissuade any others from non-compliance.

Lethal injection seems swift and relatively painless, with little to no suffering. But I am not comfortable with this idea. I am not sure it is best to choose a painless death, to avoid suffering, to make such a momentous thing so simple. I have lots to pray about. God help me!

Tuesday, October 11

Yesterday's topic was morbid and overwhelming. I didn't sleep too well last night, lots of bad dreams, anxiety, confusion, crying out, and waking up in a cold sweat. This dying stuff isn't easy. I guess nobody has ever said otherwise.

I am reminded of a section in Pilgrim's Progress where Christian and Hopeful need to cross the river to enter the Celestial City. The river stands for death. Christian and Hopeful have very different experiences. They are not able to swim, and they must walk across the river, worried about how deep it is. So, their angelic guides say to them, *"you shall find it deeper or shallower as you believe in the King of the place."* In other words, your faith in God will have a great effect on your experience of dying. Hopeful has an easy time of it. Christian despairs and says, "I sink in deep waters; the billows go over my head, all his waves go over me!" and "the sorrows of death have compassed me about!" both quotes from scripture. Christian is eventually encouraged in faith and can cross, entering the Celestial City. I must trust in God to grant me the ability to cross the river, too!

I am also reminded of the suffering of Christ in the Garden of Gethsemane. He says in Matthew 26:38, *"My soul is crushed with grief to the point of death. Stay here and keep watch with me."*[167] Jesus never seemed to lack great faith, but his death was still difficult for him. Of course, the uniqueness and intensity of his suffering, bearing the sins of the world and the holy wrath of God for them, was beyond anything we can ever comprehend. And this certainly led to his great anguish. But, nevertheless, it illustrates the point that one can suffer and struggle through death even when full of great faith. It was Jesus' concentration on what lay beyond the grave that motivated him to endure.[168]

I have been with many people on their death beds. I have seen strong believers struggle and doubt that they are going to heaven. I have seen others, not as strong, go peacefully, resting in the mercy and merits of Christ. All believers I have been with were able to hold onto some degree of faith, no matter how small and unstable. This is ultimately the work of God, not

---

[167] Matthew 26:38

[168] CF Hebrews 12:1-2, Psalm 22 etc.

ours. Ephesians 2:8 teaches us, *"God saved you by his grace when you believed. And you can't take credit for this; it is a gift from God."*[169]

I am scared about dying, but I have to rest in what God has done for me and, therefore, will continue to do. My strength, my faith, my sense of peace will not be from myself but by keeping my eyes on him. Help me, God!

Wednesday, October 12

I realized that I want to take some time to journal about technology. Believe it or not, talking about the different options for ending my life made me think of it. It seems pretty weird to be discussing technology in light of the technologies proposed to end my life. Honestly, I would rather be spending my time in person, pouring out my heartache over this whole situation, and going to God in prayer. But I believe that God wants me to press through and do my best to leave a journal that will be a help for all those who will follow after me in seeking to cling to Jesus through the trials and opportunities of this world.

So, even though it seems really morbid, the technology decisions behind my execution are a real example of the dilemma of technology – better technology doesn't necessarily lead to a better life – for one man or for all of humanity. I am reminded of the story of the Tower of Babel. You may remember it.

"[1] At one time all the people of the world spoke the same language and used the same words. [2] As the people migrated to the east, they found a plain in the land of Babylonia and settled

---

[169] Ephesians 2:8

there. ³ They began saying to each other, 'Let's make bricks and harden them with fire.' (In this region bricks were used instead of stone, and tar was used for mortar.) ⁴ Then they said, 'Come, let's build a great city for ourselves with a tower that reaches into the sky. This will make us famous and keep us from being scattered all over the world.' ⁵ But the LORD came down to look at the city and the tower the people were building. ⁶ 'Look!' he said. 'The people are united, and they all speak the same language. After this, nothing they set out to do will be impossible for them! ⁷ Come, let's go down and confuse the people with different languages. Then they won't be able to understand each other.' ⁸ In that way, the LORD scattered them all over the world, and they stopped building the city. ⁹ That is why the city was called Babel, because that is where the LORD confused the people with different languages. In this way he scattered them all over the world."¹⁷⁰

What happened is people settled in the Mesopotamian valley and made a significant advance in technology – oven-fired bricks instead of stones and tar for adhesion vs. mud. As a result, they decided to build a great tower for themselves, to reach up to heaven, to make them famous, and draw them together. The story fits into the whole storyline of Genesis, where mankind is constantly running from God and making their own way of doing things. This tower is not just about building a cool building. This tower stands for the pride and self-worship of mankind, seeking to make their own way in the world and reach the heavenly realm in their own power. Better building materials are a good thing; idolatrous mountain-like temples are not.

---

¹⁷⁰ Genesis 11:1–9

They used technology here to advance their broken and evil cause; therefore, God had to scatter mankind and keep him from cooperating on a grand scale, less such evils continue.

I share this story to illustrate how technology can go towards evil or good. Certainly, we have seen this over history in all the technologies that were developed to more efficiently kill people in war. The tremendous power of nuclear fission and fusion were developed first to destroy before they were ever used to generate electricity and environmentally friendly energy sources, such as we all have in our homes now. The lesson in this is that we can't be enamored by new technology and fail to see how it can be unhelpful and abused.

Tomorrow, I will take some time to think through examples and how I will respond to my execution options. Wow, it is really bizarre and difficult to be talking this way! Help me, O God!

Thursday, October 13

So, technology isn't always used for good. So, what are some everyday examples of this? Well, the whole area of interpersonal communications technologies is a very real example. Back in 2007, the Apple iPhone changed the world by combining a telephone with a personal computer. This allowed quick and easy access to the internet with its boundless opportunities. The innovative applications that emerged were useful for many different daily tasks and creative activities. People could track their finances, keep a calendar, read books, take amazing photos and videos and keep up with many of their friends' activities. Yet, the iPhone and its competitors were not able to replace the extensive dynamics of healthy human interaction.

The art of letter writing died off almost completely. Attention spans were reduced.[171] The ability to communicate face to face with individuals and groups was diminished.[172] Mental and physical health was shown to decline with the overuse of social media.[173] Cognitive and social maladies like ADHD[174], Bipolar

---

[171] See Carol Kinsey Goman, Has Technology Killed Face-To-Face Communication, Forbes, Nov 14, 2018,11:21am EST
https://www.forbes.com/sites/carolkinseygoman/2018/11/14/has-technology-killed-face-to-face-communication/?sh=65f38909a8cc or
Attention spans, Microsoft attention spans, Spring 2015 | @msadvertisingca, http://dl.motamem.org/microsoft-attention-spans-research-report.pdf

[172] Lucas Lengacher, Mobile Technology: Its Effect on Face-to-Face Communication and Interpersonal Interaction, Huntington University, Undergraduate Research Journal for the Human Sciences, Volume 14 – 2015

[173] See Association of Facebook Use With Compromised Well-Being: A Longitudinal Study, Holly B. Shakya, Nicholas A. Christakis, American Journal of Epidemiology, Volume 185, Issue 3, 1 February 2017, Pages 203–211, https://doi.org/10.1093/aje/kww189 or Abi-Jaoude, E., Naylor, K. T., & Pignatiello, A. (2020). Smartphones, social media use and youth mental health. CMAJ: Canadian Medical Association journal = journal de l'Association medicale canadienne, 192(6), E136–E141. https://doi.org/10.1503/cmaj.190434

[174] ADHD Throughout the Years,
https://www.cdc.gov/ncbddd/adhd/timeline.html

Disorder[175], Social Anxiety Disorder[176], Depression, Suicide[177], Pornography[178] all greatly increased during this time.[179] General happiness plunged.[180] It wasn't until a class-action lawsuit

[175] Moreno C, Laje G, Blanco C, Jiang H, Schmidt AB, Olfson M. National Trends in the Outpatient Diagnosis and Treatment of Bipolar Disorder in Youth. Arch Gen Psychiatry. 2007;64(9):1032–1039. doi:10.1001/archpsyc.64.9.103

[176] Tim Newman, Anxiety in the West: Is it on the rise?, Medical News Today, September 5, 2018,
https://www.medicalnewstoday.com/articles/322877

[177] See: Marchant A, Hawton K, Stewart A, Montgomery P, Singaravelu V, Lloyd K, et al. (2017) A systematic review of the relationship between internet use, self-harm and suicidal behavior in young people: The good, the bad and the unknown. PLoS ONE 12(8): e0181722
https://doi.org/10.1371/journal.pone.0181722

[178] See: Elwood Watson, Growing Number of People Addicted to Pornography Alarming, Diverse: Issues in Higher Education, Oct 15, 2014,
https://www.diverseeducation.com/opinion/article/15095431/growing-number-of-people-addicted-to-pornography-alarming, also See:
https://www.enough.org/stats_porn_industry and
https://www.josh.org/wp-content/uploads/Porn-Epidemic-Executive-Synopsis-9.25.2018.pdf

Oct 9, 2014 Updated Oct 15, 20

[179] Jean M. Twenge, Have Smartphones Destroyed a Generation?, The Atlantic, September, 2017, https://www.theatlantic.com/magazine/archive/2017/09/has-the-smartphone-destroyed-a-generation/534198/

[180] Jean M. Twenge, The Sad State of Happiness in the United States and the Role of Digital Media, March 20, 2019, https://worldhappiness.report/ed/2019/the-sad-state-of-happiness-in-the-united-states-and-the-role-of-digital-media/

was successfully argued before the United States Supreme Court that there was any change. That decision resulted in a ruling whereby smartphone and internet companies had to pay a tax to fund the treatment of those adversely affected by the technologies, including the terrible effects of pornography, especially sex trafficking.[181] Additionally, most governments imposed heavy taxation on the overuse of the internet and communications technology outside of regular work and school hours. Most people simply couldn't afford to be on their phones too much after this. As a result, there was a revival of many other societal and recreational pursuits. Social clubs, civic organizations, athletic associations, hobby clubs, family gatherings, and church life all saw a great renewal and deepening after this. It was as if the whole world was stuck in a weird dream and then suddenly, in a moment, woke up. Of course, communications technologies still contributed much good to society. But their abuse and detrimental effect were reduced through these changes.

This leads to my next topic – how to think about my execution options. The five options all employ different technologies – brain implants, drugs, surgery, lethal injection, or an isolation chamber. The first four are all relatively painless and, therefore, very appealing. The fifth option is likely a very difficult path towards death. But, I am thinking it is the one I should choose. I don't mean to say it is immoral to choose one of the other options. It might be in some cases. But that isn't so much what is

---

[181] See: http://www.ipjc.org/wp-content/up-loads/2016/09/USCSAHT%20-%20HT%20and%20Pornography%20module.pdf

driving me. My thought is to choose the option that does the most good, not just for my own comfort but more so in helping others and maximizing my contribution to the greater good.

Clearly, the first three options are out. They certainly would rescue me and those who love me from having to see me die physically. But they all force a spiritual and relational death on me. They do worse than that: they use my altered body and soul to create something that isn't me but something that is a robot of the state, more or less. I can't do those options. A good life and a good death are far better than those options.

Why not choose lethal injection? Well, it is appealing. It is a quick death than to glory. But is it the fullest death that I could have? Are there things I would lose in a quick death that I might gain in a slower death that gives me time to experience things and perhaps a degree of suffering that will earn a greater heavenly reward and a greater earthly impact? I am no hero, and I have no stomach for this stuff, as you have already seen. I don't want to presume on my ability to endure suffering. But I want to make sure my crossing of the river is an integral part of my whole life and my desire to optimize the goodness I might be able to produce. I think death by starvation, endured only through God's sustaining grace, is how I am to die best. I will be discussing this with Abby and some of my pastor friends. I am not totally convinced yet. But, I think this is what I am supposed to do. So, help me, God!

Friday, October 14

Well, I was allowed, even encouraged, to communicate freely with my wife, my kids, my pastor friends, and my congregants about the execution. It made for a really intense day full of lots of crying and even wailing and lots of deep sighs. It wasn't easy, and it won't be easy. Abby freaked out at the idea of not doing the lethal injection. She was horrified at the thought of me suffering until I died. She was also afraid that I would lose my sanity and end up renouncing my faith or something. I get it. But I can't make a decision based on a worst-case scenario without God in it. We were able to talk through it, and I think she saw it in the end. She had a sense of peace about it. But it took a lot of intense discussion and tears before we got there.

I had a conference call with the kids. It was even harder. Sophia was crying so much she started hyper-ventilating. Liam could barely talk because he was struggling so much. Zoey was able to talk through sobs and still carry on a conversation. Matthias, the least emotional one of the group, only needed to let his voice crack a little bit to send his other three siblings into wailing. But they were all on board pretty quickly with the possible decision. They all knew that death was more than ending your life, that it was an opportunity to trust and glorify God and leave a legacy with the living. Abby joined us at the end, and we prayed together. I keep rethinking and reliving this conversation.

My time with my pastor friends and key Christian friends was also arranged as a conference call. I had to tell them up front we would be able to say our goodbyes in person next week. The prison allows ample visiting on the last week of death row. That allowed us to get into our discussion more quickly. I am so grateful for my friends. They asked really good questions. They probed my thinking. They brought up the issues of what is moral or immoral, what is allowed versus what is preferred. They pushed me on not presuming on God's grace for death by starvation. But they also know that I have pretty good experience with the discipline of fasting for the sake of prayer and consecration. In the end, they were unanimous in supporting my decision. That was really, really helpful. My best friend, Pastor Juan, prayed for me at the end of the call. I was a basket case after that but full of peace and hope, and a deeper love for all those God has put in my life. I think I am ready to face what awaits me next week and following.

Saturday, October 15

So, I have the outline for next week. I will enter the isolation chamber at 9 am on Friday, October 21st. The chamber has ventilation, a toilet, a shower, a rubber sleeping pad and a supply of fresh drinking water, and a cup. It has an intercom should I need to speak to someone. At any point during my time there, I can call and end my isolation and starvation by choosing death by lethal injection. Also, if I do not die within 45 days, they will give me a lethal injection.

I will be allowed visitors Monday through Thursday from 9 am to 7 pm, leading up to Friday. I will be able to use the prison visitation facilities to entertain guests. The visitation facilities include a bathroom with a shower, an outdoor garden, dining facilities with meals, a living room type space, and a chapel. I can have up to 20 people at a time in the facility. It will be like staying in a cheap version of an all-expense paid hotel. I am actually very grateful for this accommodation for this important week.

Abby will be with me the whole week. The grandkids are coming on Wednesday with my mom. The kids and the pastoral team will be there on Thursday. I will have a bunch of friends from the church and otherwise coming on Monday and Tuesday. I get to sleep in the visitation facility with Abby.

This will probably be one of the most important weeks of my whole life. God, my Father, Jesus, my Savior and King, Holy Spirit, the giver and sustainer of life, come and dwell with us this coming week. Be our wisdom, our comfort, our peace, our hope, and love and joy. Be our strength. Grant us the power to trust you and glorify your worthy name. Make us a blessing to others. We ask in your name, Amen!

Sunday, October 16

I leave you with this prayer this week.[182]

Almighty God

I pray today for our brothers and sisters in Christ who are being oppressed, persecuted, and abused for their faith just as Jesus was.

Comfort and give courage to Christians throughout the world where many are experiencing physical harm, intimidation, and unjust imprisonment at the hands of their oppressors.

---

[182] Adapted from https://releaseinternational.org/prayers/a-prayer-for-the-families-of-christian-martyrs/

Our heavenly Father, thank you for welcoming into your arms all Christian martyrs who have given their lives because they refused to stop sharing the gospel and living out their faith.

Heal the hearts and minds of those who have lost loved ones because of persecution and restore them to full physical and spiritual health.

For those who persecute my brothers and sisters in Christ, I pray that their hearts will be touched by the wonderful faith of those they attack.

I pray that You will melt their hearts of ice and turn them into wellsprings of Your living water.

Through Jesus Christ our Lord, Amen.

Chapter 11: One Last Week Together

Monday, October 17

Well, this is the week. The last week of life as I have known it. Abby arrives this morning. I can't wait to see her and be with her, as hard as it is going to be. One of the hardest things about this prison sentence has been the isolation. I have sought to make the most of it by praying and reading my Bible, praying for as many people as I can remember, working through the regular offices of the day from the Book of Common Worship, and reviewing my life in prayer. Even as sweet as it has been at times to be in the Lord's presence, I still so need to be with people, especially those closest to me. Of course, Abby is the very closest and such a good friend and life partner. Truly, it is not good for humans to be alone. We are made for relationship and community, just as our God is eternally in communion as the three-in-one. And we are made in his image. I can't wait for heaven, where we will experience this without hindrance, without evil, face to face!

And I am grateful that I get to experience part of what that means as I see my dear wife and best friend today, face to face. She arrives by 9 am. Some of my closest friends from the church arrive after lunch. I will be transferring momentarily from my normal cell over to the death row visitation quarters. As much as I dread all that is coming, I am looking forward to the next four days. They are going to be really intense, but I believe God is going to be with us and also make them full of heaven as I prepare for heaven. Lots of people have been praying for me and for this time. I am really hopeful about what it will be like.

By the way, just some brief thoughts on hope. Biblical hope is often different than the usual use of the word "hope." We say things like, "I hope it doesn't rain tomorrow." or, "I hope I get that promotion." This is more a wish than a certainty. Hope is used in a wishful way in the Bible. But often, Biblical hope is the anticipation of a sure thing. We hope in what is guaranteed to come. We hope in the resurrection and the new creation in Christ. We hope in the blessings of heaven. We hope in the completion of the reign of Christ and his return.

Hope is so important. It keeps us going through the ups and downs of life. The sure hope is the most important. But it is also really important to have a reasonable temporary hope. We see this in the Apostle Paul's life. He tells the Corinthians that even though he has gone through a terrible trial that felt like death to him, this was to teach them to rely on God who raises the dead.[183] Then Paul says, "We have set our hope on the one who will deliver us again."[184] This need for deliverance was for a temporary situation. We don't know the details. It might have been a spiritual attack, it might have been persecution, it might have

---

[183] [8] We think you ought to know, dear brothers and sisters, about the trouble we went through in the province of Asia. We were crushed and overwhelmed beyond our ability to endure, and we thought we would never live through it. [9] In fact, we expected to die. But as a result, we stopped relying on ourselves and learned to rely only on God, who raises the dead. [10] And he did rescue us from mortal danger, and he will rescue us again. We have placed our confidence in him, and he will continue to rescue us. [11] And you are helping us by praying for us. Then many people will give thanks because God has graciously answered so many prayers for our safety. 2 Corinthians 1:8–11

[184] 2 Corinthians 1:10b, personal translation.

been a physical or mental illness, it might have been all of the above. It was a situation of need. And Paul was learning to put his hope in the God who raises the dead, not only for the final resurrection but also for rescue from the various trials and dangers of life.

Let me give one more example of temporary hope. In Romans 15, Paul, writing from Corinth, tells the Romans that he hopes to see them in passing as he goes to Spain. He doesn't know if he will go to Spain for sure. It is likely he did get to Spain eventually, but likely not the way he expected. There were a lot of unexpected adjustments to his plan to go to Rome and then Spain. You can read about it in Acts 20-28. It is a long story. But all along, Paul still hoped to get to Rome. Paul didn't live his life just waiting for what might come. He was a man who understood his call and made plans prayerfully. And he put hope in his plans coming to pass. He remained flexible and focused on God, but he still made plans and hoped in their outcome. This sort of hope is important to have. We can't rely on it in the way we do the hope that is guaranteed. But we are made to pray, plan and work out our best hopes for how God would use us. This sort of hope helps us keep going.

And so, this week, I am setting my hope on what is guaranteed and praying, planning, and hoping to have a week full of God's presence, power, and help as I say goodbye. Help us, O Lord. O God, who raises the dead, be with us this week and lead us in resurrection life! Amen.

Tuesday, October 18

Yesterday was almost too much to bear, and it is only the first day. I feel both totally exhausted and deeply encouraged. It turns out, those coming to visit came prepared. I thought I was going to be the one helping them when they came fully ready to help me. I am in tears thinking about the kindness and care I received yesterday. And the mastermind behind it all, of course, was my dear wife, Abby.

Juan, my best friend, and fellow pastor, visited with his wife, Susanna, and six other good friends, two couples Ryan & Grace, Oscar & Chloe, and Jonathan and Genevieve, two very dear single friends. We hugged and cried and prayed together. But probably the most uplifting thing we did was share memories together. Each one of them shared some very special memories of me as a friend or a pastor, or a co-laborer in the gospel. The memories included times as a couple, as families, and one-on-one times together. So many things have gone on in and around my life. It made me realize just how rich of a man I am.

There were funny stories, sad stories of times we walked together through trials, some of them very serious and life-altering, like when Oscar & Chloe's oldest son was killed in a car accident on his way to college. There were happy and exciting stories of times we got to see God do amazing things in our church and our community and on the mission field, like the six months Ryan & Grace, Genevieve, Abby, and I served in Indonesia, mentoring pastoral couples and watching God heal people form terminal illnesses, draw whole families and villages to himself through Bible study, and multiply churches beyond anything ever seen in history. There were stories of seasons we shared together raising kids, being part of the same house fellowship or ministry, enjoying the same hobbies, doing vacation together, and so on. It was maybe the best 4 hours with friends I have ever experienced.

And they took time in the end, one by one, to share their appreciation for me and what God had done in and through my life over the years. Probably the best thing I heard from each one of them was how God used me to show them what his strength in my weakness looks like. I have never wanted anyone to say at my funeral, "He did an amazing job!" I only want them to say, "What amazing things God did through such a needy person!"

Wednesday, October 19

I am feeling pretty emotionally and spiritually exhausted this morning. Tuesday was another really intense day. It was really, really good to spend my evening and night next to Abby. She was such a comfort to me. And I was able to comfort her and remind her of all the ways that God has answered our prayers and met us in our desperate need. I know that just as he has done that, he will do that in the coming days and coming years for Abby.

A bunch of the younger people Abby and I have mentored came yesterday. It was really sweet. And it was very encouraging to see that the church's future is in good hands, should Jesus not come back as soon as we expect. These guys are like sons and daughters to us. Some of them are not too much younger than us. Some of them are just starting out in their adult life. Abby and I have always made it a priority to mentor younger people looking to grow into their faith and develop as leaders. It has been a privilege and a pleasure for both of us. I can think of few things in life more rewarding than helping someone to become all that Jesus wants them to be.

Much of our mentoring has been simply sharing our mistakes and how God has taught us to depend so desperately on him and follow him as closely as we can. We don't have any special techniques or methods, really, beyond hanging on to Jesus as he hangs on to us. But, that is the key to everything else, for in him dwells all the fullness of God,[185] in him are all the treasures of wisdom and knowledge[186], in him his fathomless love![187]

Each of our younger friends took the time to encourage Abby and me and share their gratitude. Many of them shared specific scriptures with their sense of what the Holy Spirit was emphasizing for me to hear. It was very powerful and very encouraging. Sheila, a missionary friend who served for many years in very difficult circumstances, shared from 2 Corinthians 1, totally unaware of how important this verse has been for me these past months. She shared that she felt God wanted to

---

[185] For God in all his fullness was pleased to live in Christ,

Colossians 1:19

[186] In him lie hidden all the treasures of wisdom and knowledge. Colossians 2:3,

[187] May you experience the love of Christ, though it is too great to understand fully. Then you will be made complete with all the fullness of life and power that comes from God. Ephesians 3:19,

remind Abby and me that he is the God who raises the dead. We are to fully rely on the God who doesn't leave his people in the valley of the shadow of death but raises them to life. Wow, did that hit home! Sheila even shared a sense that this would be the truth that God would use to strengthen me for what lies ahead.

DeShawn shared Hebrews 12:1-2.[188] He looked straight at me, and with tear-filled eyes and such a sincere face, told me great joy awaited me, the greatest being my Savior waiting for me at the finish line. I can still vividly see the face of my very dear friend – a handsome, masculine African American man, shining with the wisdom and the love of Christ. I can't believe I got to help this man, and many like him, become bishops in the church.

I wish I had more time to write about the many others who shared and encouraged me. I am grateful for Isabella, Shanice, Annisa & Gunadi, Scott & Linda, Matt & Gayle, Seo-yeon, Hamza & Yalina, Mateo, Min-seo, Diego & Sharon, Tyrone, Logan & Jasmine, Bao & Ju, and all the others we weren't able to see yesterday. I love you guys so much. I will be praying for you until the Lord takes me. It has been such a privilege to be your friend and mentor. I feel so supported. Thank you, God!

---

[188] "Therefore, since we are surrounded by such a huge crowd of witnesses to the life of faith, let us strip off every weight that slows us down, especially the sin that so easily trips us up. And let us run with endurance the race God has set before us. We do this by keeping our eyes on Jesus, the champion who initiates and perfects our faith. Because of the joy awaiting him, he endured the cross, disregarding its shame. Now he is seated in the place of honor beside God's throne." Hebrews 12:1–2

Thursday, October 20

Today is a big day. This is my last day of visitation. I wish this could go on for a long time. I am glad that will be the case in heaven. Today the kids will be here along with Abby. The other pastors will come for a final visit and worship service right before dinner. I am full of longing for our time and dread about what is ahead. Help me, Lord, with this overwhelming mix of contradictory feelings.

It was so good to see my mom yesterday, along with the grandkids. My mom is struggling with my imprisonment and sentence. Part of the problem is her dementia. It is not severe but has affected her ability to process new situations and new information. Many things are confusing and overwhelming for her, especially something so serious as my death sentence. She also struggles with our stand on this issue. She is confused as to why we can't just be more careful with what we say and do to stay out of trouble with the government. She doesn't understand how strict, intrusive and unyielding they are on these issues of Christian conscience. She also doesn't understand that it isn't something we can change, given it is an issue of being silent not only in our witness to Christ in our community but also with our own people. We can't make a Jesus and a Christianity that will bow its knee to this or any other government. It isn't about pride; it is about core truth and life, including eternal life.

Even so, my Madrecita was amazingly understanding and supportive. She told me, like she always has, that I am the best son, and she loves me, "¡Te amo tanto, Lucasito!" I will miss hearing those words. I told her how much I love her and how grateful I am for all that she and Dad did for me and for us. What wonderful parents God gave me! I am looking forward to seeing Dad. I am so glad that they put their trust in Jesus and will be by my side as I worship in heaven. Though, I think my mom will have a front-row seat. She spent so many hours praying for others and caring for the needy in our church. She is a grandmother to probably hundreds of people. I love you, Amá!

Oh boy, it's gonna be hard to write and relive the time with the grandkids. Marie, our firstborn grandchild, was so wise and godly. She had tears in her eyes but was focused on encouraging me and her grandmother and her parents. She said that all those promises and all those stories in the Bible are for us at this time. All the truth, all the comfort, all the power of those stories are there for us to draw real strength in this time of deepest need. She looked at me with tears and an intense face and said, "Abue, don't you forget who is on your side! Don't you forget you are surrounded by billions of brothers and sisters! Don't you forget that God himself is with you! Please, don't forget!" Wow. I am crying writing it now. I told her I couldn't promise that, but I can promise he won't forget me and that is all my hope. And I told her that he will help me remember, and he will use her strong reminder for me. There is no way I will forget that face and those words!

And my two grandsons of thunder, John and Luke, told me with grit that God was gonna take care of all the bad guys and make everything right in the end. They told me that I was their hero and Jesus was gonna reward me for not giving up and doing so many things for him. I said, "Thanks, my grandsons of thunder, May God give you faith to stand firm in him!" I also told them that Abue's confidence is in the only real hero, Jesus. And he is always with us. I told them I was gonna miss them but that we would have lots of time together in heaven, so don't be sad.

There were lots of hugs and kisses with the younger ones. We got to read books together, sing songs, and worship all together as an extended family. They all prayed for me, including Saphia as well. It was such a sweet time and full of many tears – tears of gratitude, tears of love, tears of sorrow. We talked about lots of things together, too. We talked about school, science, art, sports. We talked about church. We talked about God and his kingdom. The kids were mesmerized as I told them some of my thoughts on what the final kingdom might be like. I believe the thought of being able to transport ourselves across space instantaneously was super cool for them. I don't know if it will work that way, but it seems Jesus did that in his resurrection body. We talked about playing intergalactic tag. Aafreen, Zana, and Evelyn got the giggles with that, probably a mix of nerves and the funny idea of Abue chasing them across galaxies. It was good for our souls.

Before they left, we all got down on our knees and spent time thanking God for as many things as we could think about. Soroush, the profound one, said, "Thank you, God, for this opportunity for Abue to get even closer to Jesus through sharing in his sufferings." Thank God for my amazing grandson. Oh Jesus, help me to get so close to you as I suffer! I need you. I want to be with you! I can only do this if you are very, very, very near to me! Fulfill my grandson's prayer. Thank you for him. Keep him ever close to you, Jesus!

There was even more that was said and experienced, but I think I was able to capture it. I am more grateful now for my extended family than I have ever been. What a rich man I am! Thank you, God!

Now, help us as we face our final full day of visiting and our last night together as a couple. We know you will be with us. Thank you, Amen. I leave you with this evening prayer:

Compline[189]

Leader:	*Father, Son, Holy Spirit, I welcome you here.*
	The light is gone, the dark is here.
	This night, each night, may I know the light of Your presence.
	Thank you Father, that you have said you will never leave me or forsake me.
Leader:	*Where I have failed to walk in the path you have set before me.*
All:	*Father, forgive.*
Leader:	*When the world has worn me down.*
All:	*Jesus, restore.*
Leader:	*Where I have looked to my own strength rather than your strength.*

---

[189] Pete Ward, https://www.24-7prayer.com/officescompline

All:	*Spirit, renew.*
	Lord, I surrender myself into your hands.
Leader:	*Those for whom I am praying and the situations I am anxious for you to be at work in.*
All:	*I release them into your hands.*
Leader:	*Those whose lives I long to see transformed by the experience of your salvation,*
All:	*I release them into your hands.*
Leader:	*Those peoples and situations that urgently require your justice,*
All:	*I release them into your hands.*
Leader:	*Lord, all of my concerns I give to you.*
	Your yoke is easy, and your burden is light.
All:	*Draw me near this night, Lord Jesus,*
Leader:	*Your presence sustains me.*
	Hide me in the shadow of your wings,
All:	*Draw me near Lord Jesus.*
Leader:	*May thoughts of your wonders fill my dreams,*
	Draw me near Lord Jesus.
All:	*Leader: That I might come to tomorrow refreshed,*
	Draw me near Lord Jesus.

Leader:	*Ready for the working or for the resting that you would put me to,*
All:	*Draw me near this night, Lord Jesus.*
Leader:	*Father, Son, Holy Spirit, be with me as I rest in You this night.*

Amen

Friday, October 21

Well, this is my last entry. It is 8:30 am. Abby just left. They will be coming to get me in 30 minutes – just enough time for my final entry. There is so much I could say, but I have said a lot over the past two months. Before I share my final thoughts, let me recount how yesterday and this morning went.

Abby and I have been doing morning worship and prayer together every morning. We have taken time to work through the morning, noon, evening, and compline offices from the Book of Common Worship. We have added to it our own hymns from memory. It has been such a taste of heaven to sing and harmonize with the most beautiful voice I know. And it has been so good to recite the prayers and scripture readings that billions of my brothers and sisters have used for centuries. This has calmed our souls tremendously. We know that many have gone before us, have tasted death, even martyrdom, and are awaiting us now in the presence of God himself. This life is but a blip, and its trials are only light momentary afflictions compared to the eternal weight of glory that is soon to be seen and experienced.

The kids arrived early. It was just the kids. The grandkids were at home. I love my kids so much. One of the hardest things for me is to trust God for them that they will endure to the end, that they will make the most of their lives, that they will avoid falsehoods and tantalizing half-truths, that they will be there with us to enjoy God forever. But I must trust God and not myself. I must dethrone my will and know God is good and more than able to keep them for that final reward. How silly to think that I am able to do really anything for them apart from God!

Matthias and Isabella, Zoey and Arman, Sophia and Liam, Abby and I were alone together through lunchtime. I took time to tell each one of them how grateful I am for them and how proud I am of them. There are so many things about them I treasure, so many character qualities, personality aspects, gifts, and skills that are such blessings. There are so many things they have done and are doing that are praiseworthy. I am so glad that Abby and I learned the habit of focusing most of our interaction with the kids on gratitude and praise while they were still young. This has borne much fruit over the years, especially in our own hearts.

They took time to honor Abby and me. Each of them had written a letter to M

om and me. If I had longer to live, I would frame each of those letters and hang them in my office and read and reread them each day. They were holy words and so precious. That hour or so listening to each of them (couples together) read and interact with us over their letters was so awesome. It felt like mighty angels were in our midst, and God the Holy Spirit was visiting us with great power. We prayed, we wept, we sang, we laid hands on each other, and we asked God for grace and power to endure and serve in this trying time. I strongly believe our children will be instrumental in helping to lead the church through her finest hour.

The elders arrived a little before dinner. They had a complete worship time planned out, with readings, encouragements, personal sharing, music, and both planned and spontaneous prayer. Unbeknownst to me, they had planned and obtained permission to broadcast the last 30 minutes of the worship time exclusively to the whole church. Pastor Juan led us in taking communion together, us in prison and the congregation, gathered at the parish church building, under the leadership of Pastor Che. I was a blubbering mess that couldn't even form a coherent word but just took the elements with my wife's hand in mine and before all those smiling faces full of tears. I can't imagine anything closer to heaven. We closed with the old and wonderful hymn, "Holy, Holy, Holy," sung acapella in four parts. It was so heavenly.

We had final prayers together, and the elders laid hands on me and prayed earnestly, with tears, for me, that I would have the strength to endure, that I would know God's powerful presence, that I would be a strong witness to the life and truth of Christ in a dark world. We said goodbye with hugs that were hard to end.

Next, we said goodbye to the kids. This was really, really hard. Everybody was speechless with grief yet full of joy and hope in Christ. We prayed together, hugged forever, kissed, blessed each other in the name of the Father, Son, and Holy Spirit, and said our final goodbye. Oh boy.

I had asked the kids to bring some floral arrangements and gifts for Abby for our last meal and evening together. We also had requested her favorite meal: Clam Chowder, Cobb Salad, Boiled Lobster, Steak, and an IPA Beer. It was the best meal I ever had, I think. The hydrangeas and orchid arrangements were dazzling and transformed the room with their beauty and smells. And I got Abby some special jewelry, including her favorite stone, sapphires to match her eyes. She put it on right away. The necklace and earrings, and headband looked so beautiful on her. I love that woman and her beautiful face full of so much love, wisdom, and life. If it weren't for the sure promise I will see her again, I would completely fall apart. We enjoyed lots of time together rehearsing the major events of our lives, all that God did in and around us, all the things we are grateful to have received. We prayed for all the things we want to see in our kids, our church, and in the whole world. We felt such peace together as we did this. I think Abby was finally able to let go. The tension in her face broke. She cried and cried and cried and then started laughing with joy. She said that she got it. That it truly was going to be all right and even better because of all that is going on. She had such a powerful encounter with God in our time. She knew he had it all in his hands and would truly fulfill his promise to work it out for the ultimate good.[190] It is one thing to know this promise. It is another to feel it deep in your soul and body. That is what happened with Abby. I am so glad for this answer to prayer.

---

[190] "And we know that God causes everything to work together for the good of those who love God and are called according to his purpose for them." Romans 8:28

Abby and I enjoyed the last time of intimacy together, and we thanked God for the tremendous blessing of our union and our sex life. We professed our trust in God to fulfill the promise of a greater union in Christ, even though we are not sure how it will all work out. We know it will be infinitely better and fuller, even though no longer a coital union.

I didn't sleep too well last night. My life-long struggle with panic attacks resurfaced. It starts with a dark thought that seems to trigger me spiritually and emotionally, and then my body reacts in panic, and I spiral downward into overwhelming and irrational anxiety. The dark thought last night was, again, "Isn't this just your pride? Aren't you ruining everybody's lives because of your foolish pride? You are gonna cause irreparable harm and eternal darkness because of this!" The thought wasn't that coherent, but more or less, that's what it was. I started to go into a downward spiral, but Sheila's encouragement that we must rely on God, who raises the dead, started to fill my thoughts. I focused on that truth and pictured myself being resurrected along with all God's people and worshipping in the New Jerusalem. It was a vivid picture in my mind's eye, and I found the anxiety and panic and flush of emotion lifting. It happened a couple more times but remembering 2 Corinthians 1:9 and picturing it in my mind worked each time. Thankfully, I was able to get some sleep before we woke up at 6 AM.

This morning, after a light breakfast, we prayed and kissed and hugged and cried over and over again. The guard had to come in and tell us it was time for Abby to go. It was like trying to pull apart two powerful magnets. Our last point of physical touch was our fingertips. Our last sight was looking into each other's tear-filled eyes full of love and trust in our good God.

I'm so glad that God has given us the strength to say goodbye for now. As incredibly heart-wrenching as it is, we feel miraculously buoyed to endure this. Thank you, God!!!

Now, for my final words. I don't need to say much. There are lots of things I could say. But, I want to say only what is most necessary. It is simply this:

Cling to Jesus Christ, God in the Flesh, crucified and risen for your salvation, as Jesus, your Savior, and King, clings to you and never lets go. Amen.

I love you guys so much, Abby, the kids, the grandkids, Amá, my extended family, my dear church friends, and so many more. I will see you on the other side. May God bless all who read this, the confessions of a 21st-Century martyr.

Your friend, Lucas Sullivan.

Chapter 12: Only the Beginning

My dad went into that isolation cell on that Friday, October 21st. He lasted all 45 days and he died from lethal injection on December 7th, just a week ago. We buried him yesterday. His body awaits the final resurrection alongside many others in the parish cemetery plot. It has been incredibly hard to lose Dad but I can't imagine a better way to go.

Dad remained faithful to the end. He had some hard moments I'm sure, but he never opted out of death by starvation. It was amazing he went the whole 45 days. One of the guards got word out, secretly, that Dad spent a lot of time singing and reciting scripture and speaking the various liturgies out loud. He also said that he constantly was asking the guards how he could pray for them and exhorting them to trust in Jesus. He also shared very honestly with them how much he struggled and doubted but also how God met him in those struggles. The guard who reported all this was so affected by my dad that he came to faith in Christ himself and is planning to get baptized next week.

My dad had an amazing life. He got to live through what is probably the most amazing time in history, where so many of the promises of God for the church have been fulfilled. We have seen the Kingdom of God come in such a powerful way, yet still await its completion. Only then, upon Christ's return and final judgement, will we know its fullness. We must live in the "already and not yet" of the Kingdom of God.[191] As much as we can pray and yearn and work for the advancement of the kingdom in our lifetimes, we must set our ultimate hope on the future and final kingdom. I can't wait to be there with Dad in the presence of God and all his people.

But now we await what will likely be the final days before Christ's return. We are not sure, but there are enough biblical signs to indicate it may be very soon: 1) the Great Commission has been fulfilled, with vibrant disciples in churches in every village in the world,[192] 2) the harvest of the Jewish people has taken place with so many coming to faith in their Messiah,[193] 3)

---

[191] CF: Ladd, G. E. (1994). The gospel of the Kingdom. Wm. B. Eerdmans Publishing Company.

[192] "Jesus came and told his disciples, 'I have been given all authority in heaven and on earth. Therefore, go and make disciples of all the nations, baptizing them in the name of the Father and the Son and the Holy Spirit. Teach these new disciples to obey all the commands I have given you. And be sure of this: I am with you always, even to the end of the age.' " (Matthew 28:18–20)

[193] "12 Now if the Gentiles were enriched because the people of Israel turned down God's offer of salvation, think how much greater a blessing the world will share when they finally accept it. 13 I am saying all this especially for you Gentiles. God has appointed me as the apostle to the Gentiles. I stress this, 14 for I want somehow to make the people of Israel jealous of what you Gentiles have, so I might save some of them. 15 For since their rejection meant that God offered salvation to the rest of the world, their acceptance will be even more wonderful. It will be life for those who were dead!... 25 I want you to understand this mystery, dear brothers and sisters, so that you will not feel proud about yourselves. Some of the people of Israel have hard hearts, but this will last only until the full number of Gentiles comes to

the whole church has reached a maturity that is truly amazing, displaying a unity, doctrinal integrity and fruitfulness on a scale only dreamed of previously,[194] 4) the new world-wide government has set itself up as the ultimate authority and the new supreme leader has declared himself as a reincarnation of Christ himself and arranged for his own world-wide worship based in the reconstructed temple in Jerusalem,[195] 5) Christians

---

Christ. [26] And so all Israel will be saved. As the Scriptures say, "The one who rescues will come from Jerusalem, and he will turn Israel away from ungodliness. [27] And this is my covenant with them, that I will take away their sins."

Romans 11:12-15, 25-27

[194] "[11] Now these are the gifts Christ gave to the church: the apostles, the prophets, the evangelists, and the pastors and teachers. [12] Their responsibility is to equip God's people to do his work and build up the church, the body of Christ. [13] This will continue until we all come to such unity in our faith and knowledge of God's Son that we will be mature in the Lord, measuring up to the full and complete standard of Christ." Ephesians 4:11–13

"[7] Let us be glad and rejoice, and let us give honor to him. For the time has come for the wedding feast of the Lamb, and his bride has prepared herself. [8] She has been given the finest of pure white linen to wear." For the fine linen represents the good deeds of God's holy people." Revelation 19:7–8

[195] "[1] Now, dear brothers and sisters, let us clarify some things about the coming of our Lord Jesus Christ and how we will be gathered to meet him. [2] Don't be so easily shaken or alarmed by those who say that the day of the Lord has already begun. Don't believe them, even if they claim to have had a spiritual vision, a revelation, or a letter supposedly from us. [3] Don't be fooled by what they say. For that day will not come until there is a great rebellion against God and the man of lawlessness is revealed – the one who brings destruction. [4] He will exalt himself and defy everything that people

have been excluded from every aspect of life, imprisoned by the thousands, threatened with death, some denying the faith and betraying their brothers and sisters. [196, 197]

Whether or not Christ returns soon, we will endure by his grace. Even now, as we hear so many terrible stories of persecution and evil, we hear many more of heroism, faithfulness to Christ in the face of hatred, we hear of love, care and mercy for others, even the persecutors. We see all around us an incredible strength and resiliency among God's people, not because they are strong but because they are holding on to the one who is stronger than any other. May God be glorified in the

---

call god and every object of worship. He will even sit in the temple of God, claiming that he himself is God. [5] Don't you remember that I told you about all this when I was with you?" 2 Thessalonians 2:1–5

[196] [9] "Then you will be arrested, persecuted, and killed. You will be hated all over the world because you are my followers. [10] And many will turn away from me and betray and hate each other. [11] And many false prophets will appear and will deceive many people. [12] Sin will be rampant everywhere, and the love of many will grow cold. [13] But the one who endures to the end will be saved. [14] And the Good News about the Kingdom will be preached throughout the whole world, so that all nations will hear it; and then the end will come." Matthew 24:9–14

[197] [11] "Then I saw another beast come up out of the earth. He had two horns like those of a lamb, but he spoke with the voice of a dragon. [12] He exercised all the authority of the first beast. And he required all the earth and its people to worship the first beast, whose fatal wound had been healed…[16] He required everyone – small and great, rich and poor, free and slave – to be given a mark on the right hand or on the forehead. [17] And no one could buy or sell anything without that mark, which was either the name of the beast or the number representing his name." Revelation 13:11-12,16–17

faithfulness and fruitfulness of his church, even amidst terrible persecutions and trials!

We eagerly await the day when Christ shall appear and rent the skies, when his saints rise from the dead to greet him and welcome him to his earthly reign. We live for that final day, the day of judgement of all mankind, when the books will be opened and each judged for his or her works. Those who have trusted Christ and displayed the righteousness of faith will be welcomed into eternal reward. Those who have rejected the constant kindness and patience of God will receive the just wrath of such evil. Then all will bend their knees and confess that Jesus Christ is Lord. And he will be eternally exalted as King as he turns his final kingdom over to the Father and we enjoy eternal bliss in a new creation.

Then, as CS Lewis once said about the end,

> "...but the things that began to happen after that were so great and beautiful that I cannot write them. And for us this the end of all the stories, and we can most truly say that they all lived happily ever after. But for them it was only the beginning of the real story. All their life in this world and all their adventures in Narnia [Lewis' fictional world] had only been the cover and the title page: now at last they were beginning Chapter One of the Great Story which no one on earth has read: which goes on forever: in which every chapter is better than the one before."[198]

---

[198] The Last Battle by CS Lewis © copyright CS Lewis Pte Ltd 1956. Extract used with permission. p. 228

So it shall be as seen so vividly throughout God's word. I leave you with this passage that has sustained and propelled us. It is what soon awaits all the faithful. It has inspired countless believers. May it inspire you too!

> "9 And they sang a new song with these words: "You are worthy to take the scroll and break its seals and open it. For you were slaughtered, and your blood has ransomed people for God from every tribe and language and people and nation. 10 And you have caused them to become a Kingdom of priests for our God. And they will reign on the earth." 11 Then I looked again, and I heard the voices of thousands and millions of angels around the throne and of the living beings and the elders. 12 And they sang in a mighty chorus: "Worthy is the Lamb who was slaughtered – to receive power and riches and wisdom and strength and honor and glory and blessing." 13 And then I heard every creature in heaven and on earth and under the earth and in the sea. They sang: "Blessing and honor and glory and power belong to the one sitting on the throne and to the Lamb forever and ever." 14 And the four living beings said, "Amen!" And the twenty-four elders fell down and worshiped the Lamb."

Revelation 5:9–14

Made in the USA
Columbia, SC
03 September 2022

66621451R00122